SKULDUGGERY

Anne Adeney

Illustrated by Wendy Smith

Galaxy

CHIVERS PRESS
BATH

First published 1999
as a Dolphin paperback
by
Orion Children's Books
This Large Print edition published by
Chivers Press
by arrangement with
Orion Children's Books
2002

ISBN 0 7540 6195 7

British Library Cataloguing in Publication Data

Adeney, Anne
Skulduggery.—Large print ed.
1. Detective and mystery stories. 2. Children's stories
3. Large type books
I. Title II. Smoth, Wendy
823.9'12[J]

ISBN 0-7540-6195-7

Printed and bound in Great Britain by
BOOKCRAFT, Midsomer Norton, Somerset

To my husband Richard,
with much love
A.A.

Contents

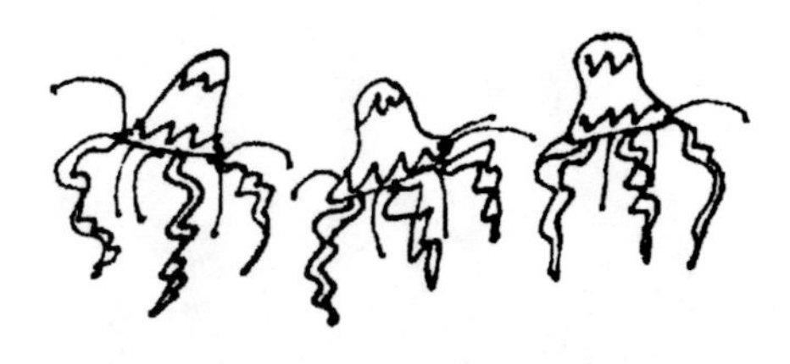

Contents

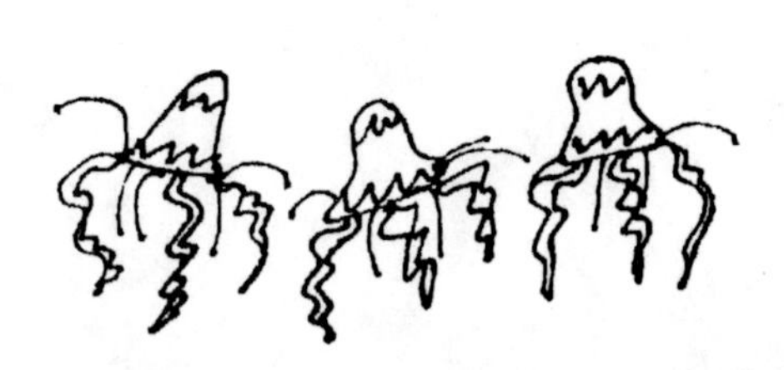

CHAPTER ONE

A SCREAM IN THE NIGHT

The scream echoed eerily in the still night. The sound was so horrible, so scary, that Tim felt the hairs on the back of his neck stand up and brush the collar of his pyjama jacket. The towel he had been using dropped unnoticed to the floor. Unconsciously, he rubbed his wet hands down the front of his pyjamas.

Then he stood, limpet-like, unable to move, for several long seconds. His head ached from the effort of trying to listen, trying to tune in his ears to the middle of the night sounds. All was silent in the sleeping house.

He let out his breath in a long whoosh before turning quickly to click on the light switch. He hadn't bothered before. He never did when he got up in the night. There was a light on in the hall anyway, so he just left the bathroom door open a bit. His little sister almost always got up and wandered into Mum and Dad's room at some point in the night so the light was left on for her.

Tim shook his head. Jumping jellyfish! He must have imagined it. He had certainly been half asleep when he'd stumbled into the bathroom. He must still have been dreaming. But he frowned as he reached up to get his glass from the shelf, turning on the cold tap as he did so. Why should there be a scream in his dream?

He'd been having a brilliant dream, where he was a marine biologist like his father. He'd been with him down in the cold Antarctic seas, sharing his work, charting his observations. Now *that* was his idea of a perfect summer holiday. Not stuck at home without his dad for months. No camping or hiking to look forward to. Only the awful prospect of extra work with a tutor to improve his reading.

In his dream they'd just drawn a sample of plankton into the boat and were about to analyse it and record their findings when the urgent need to use the bathroom had woken Tim up. It must have been all those huge Antarctic waves pounding against the side of their research ship. Water always seemed to have that effect on him, even imagined water.

Tim sighed deeply. His father had been away on his research trip for two long months now, eight and a half weeks, fifty-nine days. Tim took a quick look at his watch. It was 3 a.m. He multiplied quickly. He was good at maths. Dad had been away one thousand, five hundred and twenty-nine hours. Ninety-one thousand, seven hundred and forty-two minutes. He sighed again. He ought to be used to it after all this time. He wished he could crawl into bed with Mum like Frannie did every night. But he was eleven, too old for that now.

He gulped down the cold water and turned off the tap. Good job Mum wasn't awake. She'd tell him off for leaving the tap running for so long. She was all for saving the planet's resources, and water was precious in the summer, especially here in the South West.

As the sound of running water ceased, Tim's ears were shocked into alertness once more. Had that been the tail-end of another scream? He shook the last drops of water from his glass and held it against the bathroom wall, pressing his ear to the base.

'No! No! Please don't hurt me!' came a woman's agonised wail from the other side of the wall. 'I'd tell you everything, but I just don't know! I don't know where it is, please believe me!'

Another long drawn-out howl made Tim's ears sing and suddenly his whole body was shaking. Something truly *horrible* was going on next door.

It was their nasty neighbour, that awful Mr Wizer. Tim had been suspicious of him for months now. He might have known he'd be up to no good. Mr Wizer hated children, particularly boys, and especially Tim. He hated animals, particularly cats, and especially Tim's cat, Minty. He even hated the sunshine, and had kept his curtains drawn tightly shut all through the hot, dry summer.

Mr Wizer had a flat on the upstairs floor of the terraced house next to Tim. The room on the other side of the bathroom must be his bedroom, or maybe his living room. It sounded as if he was actually *torturing* someone in there, trying to make her tell him something. Almost against his will, Tim pressed his ear to the glass again, trying desperately to control his shaking hand.

'No! No! Not the knife! Please don't cut my face! You know I'm a model. My face is my whole life! Please don't cut my face!'

'It's not your face you should be worried about, sweetheart, it's your throat! Tell me where it is or your next breath will be your last!'

The voice was thick and gruff and

No no!!

horribly menacing. Mr Wizer obviously meant every word of it! Tim dropped the glass, threw open the door and bounded down the stairs in three gigantic leaps. It was no good trying to wake Mum. She slept like a log and took a good five minutes to wake up, even in an emergency. Tim and Frannie had learnt at a very early age that lying in bed howling was a waste of time if they woke in the middle of the night. The only thing to do was to go and get into bed with her.

So Tim knew better than to waste time telling her what was going on. He must get the police before the poor woman next door was murdered! His hands were shaking so much that he dropped the phone twice before his trembling finger found the number 9 button and pressed it three times.

'Which service do you require, police, fire or ambulance?' came the calm voice from the other end of the telephone.

'Police! Get me the police, quickly! Mr Wizer is murdering a lady next door! If you don't come quickly he'll cut her throat!' Tim's voice was surprisingly firm.

'A car will be on its way immediately. Just give me your name and address please, madam.'

Tim was too relieved to be annoyed that someone had taken him for a female. It was probably a good thing anyway. Police always took much more notice of an adult.

'Err . . . it's Mrs Maria Randolph of 28 Gladstone Place, in Plymouth—near the crossroads in Mutley. The murderer is my neighbour, Mr Wizer. He lives next door, at number 30. It's the very end house on the terrace, the upstairs flat. Do come quickly, he's killing somebody!'

'A car is in your vicinity, Mrs Randolph, and we are in radio contact. They will be with you in minutes. Do not attempt to approach this man yourself. Stay indoors until the police arrive. Is the man armed?'

'Yes, he's got a knife and he's going to cut her throat! You must stop him!'

Abruptly Tim hung up the phone. What if it was too late? He should have

rung the police after that very first scream. What if stopping to work out how many hours and minutes Dad had been away and getting that cold drink had meant the difference between life and death for that poor woman? Mr Wizer was the murderer, but might not he, Tim Randolph, also be to blame?

CHAPTER TWO

MINTY IS MISSING

Tim tiptoed down the back stairs and peeped into the kitchen. If only he hadn't dropped his cycle helmet on the floor yesterday when he came in. He could see it there in the corner where he'd kicked it. If only he'd hung it up in the hall as he was meant to. Then he could have just grabbed it as he ran through the front door, yelling goodbye as he went. He could have been on his bike and well away before Mum caught up with him.

Mum was sighing as she slapped her new diet sheet onto the tall door of the fridge and secured it with a pig-shaped magnet. The pig had a balloon coming out of its mouth with the words, 'Eat a carrot, you fat pig!' written on it.

Mum was usually on a diet, and her magnet collection was supposed to help her stop eating. Tim thought her shape was perfectly fine for a mother, and wished she wouldn't bother, especially when she stopped baking cakes and biscuits in an effort to lose weight. He'd rather have a piece of cake than a carrot, any day.

He turned to creep away again, then froze as he heard Mum's voice.

'Is that you, Tim? Where do you think you're off to? I've got jobs I want doing.'

Tim came reluctantly into the kitchen. 'But Mum, I *can't*! Not today! It's Joseph's last day before he goes on holiday. He staying on his Grandad's farm for the whole of the summer holidays, and I won't see him again until September! We planned to cycle right through Plym Bridge Woods and then go swimming. They're having a barbecue in their back garden and I was going to sleep over for his last night. You know about that. You *said* I could go. I won't have time to do any extra jobs today!'

Mum started to turn puce. She looked as if she was about to explode. Tim took a step backwards.

'I'll do them tomorrow, I promise,' he began.

'How dare you, Timothy Randolph! How dare you? After what you've done! After all you've put me through! I've had the police traipsing through my house in the middle of the night, accusing me, accusing *me,* of hoax calls on an innocent neighbour! You do *know* what a hoax is, don't you, Timothy? It's a mean, spiteful, practical joke.'

Tim winced. 'I'm sorry about the police, really I am, Mum! How was I to know he was watching a video? *Normal* people don't watch videos in the middle of the night! Not after 3 o'clock in the morning, anyway. I was going to give my name, really I was. But they thought I was you. So I thought I'd better go along with it, especially after last time . . . '

Tim's voice trailed away. He could almost see the inside of Mum's brain running 'last time' through like a newsreel. Why had he even mentioned it?

Last time had been just over a week ago. His cat, Minty, had been missing for ages. She was a lazy, homeloving cat, who liked nothing better than to curl up on someone's knee and be stroked to sleep. She never went very far from the house. She certainly wasn't the roving type.

But Minty was in the habit of using the garden at the back of Mr Wizer's house as her toilet. She always had done. Everyone knows that cats never go in their own garden. Mr Wizer was always swearing at Minty, and at Tim for not controlling her. As if you could control where a cat decides to go!

It was not even as if there was anything in Mr Wizer's garden that she could harm. The garden really belonged to the flat on the ground floor, and that was always taken by students. They never bothered to do anything in the garden except sunbathe. But Mr Wizer always swore he would kill Minty if he could get hold of her.

So when Minty disappeared, Tim naturally worried that Mr Wizer had got her. Then, one day when he came home from school, there was a terrible smell coming from next door. Tim rushed to Dad's study which looked out over the garden.

Thick black smoke was spiralling from an old tin drum in the next door garden. Flames licked fiercely over the edges. Trailing down the side of the drum Tim could see a long piece of black fur. He *knew* it was Minty's tail. Mum had still been out at work and he knew there wasn't time to explain the whole story about Minty to Mrs Trump, who looked after them. He had phoned the RSPCA and the police at once and they'd come pretty quickly to investigate.

The black fur had turned out to be part of a lady's coat that Mr Wizer had been burning. Tim had heard the police tell him not to burn things like that in the garden because of the pollution. So he had taken the rest of his stuff back indoors. But when Mum came home she found both the RSPCA and the police giving Tim a stern warning about making accusations without any proof.

Tim always felt they'd gone away without investigating things thoroughly. If *he'd* been a detective, he'd have made a much better job of it. Why did Mr Wizer have a woman's coat in the first place? He lived alone. He had no wife or girlfriend that anyone had ever seen. Then again, why was he burning the coat in the garden? Everyone knows fur smells awful when you burn it. If he wanted to get rid of it, why didn't he just put it in the bin, or give it to a charity shop?

Tim was sure that Mr Wizer had bought the coat, and burnt it just when he knew Tim would be coming home from school. He knew how worried Tim was about his cat, because he'd even asked him if he'd seen Minty. The whole thing was organised to upset Tim, to get his own back for Minty going in his garden. Tim was convinced of that. But he'd had no luck convincing anyone else, particularly Mum.

'Oh yes, I remember last time too, Timothy. You were making accusations again! Unfounded accusations! You can't go cycling with Joseph anyway, because you have to visit the police station with me. As if it isn't bad enough that I've had such a disturbed night I'll hardly be able to function at work! No, I've also got to take time off to take you down to the police station!

You really are the limit! I don't know what your father is going to say about this, I really don't.'

'You're not going to *tell* him, are you Mum? You're not going to tell Dad?'

Tim's voice was breaking with tears now, despite his efforts to control it. Dad was out on his research ship most of the time, so he was only able to telephone them about once a fortnight when he got back to base. Even that was on a crackly radio phone, where you had to keep remembering to say 'over' every time you stopped talking. Mum *couldn't* be going to waste those few precious moments telling Dad about this! It was only a misunderstanding after all. It wasn't as if he'd done something awful on *purpose*.

Mum sighed loudly, but tactfully didn't mention the tears, although Tim knew she'd seen them. She poured out two glasses of squash and put them

down on the kitchen table. She sat down and patted the chair beside her.

'Come and sit down here, Tim. It's so hot I'm sure we're both ready for a drink. And I think we need to have a talk. No, I'm not going to tell Dad, not now. But I'll expect you to tell him about it yourself when he gets home and you've got time to explain the whole thing properly. I know you *meant* well. But you just don't seem to appreciate the trouble you've caused.'

'I do, really I do, Mum! I'll never phone the police again, I promise. Not even if I think we're being burgled!'

'Like the time you attacked the man who came to collect the things I'd left out for the charity shop!'

'Oh, Mum! I didn't *attack* him. And I didn't call the police then, either. I just asked him what he was doing. You know Dad told me to look after you and Frannie while he was away. I *am* the man of the house now, that's what he said.'

There were tears in Mum's eyes as she hugged him hard. He knew how much she missed Dad too.

'After this last escapade you'd better consider yourself grounded for a few days. But we'll say no more about it. Just remember I'm relying on you to be sensible. *Think* before you do anything. I'm sure you must be watching too much TV. The sort of things you keep imagining just don't happen to people like us!'

'Well, they have to happen to someone, don't they? It's always on the News and on things like *Crimewatch.'*

'*Crimewatch!* When have you ever watched that? It's on really late at night! That's not a suitable thing for you to watch! Tim, tell me the truth. Have you ever crept down to watch programmes like *Crimewatch*? Maybe when Dad and I were out and Mrs Trump was busy in the kitchen?'

Tim shook his head hard. 'Never, Mum, I promise.' He thought it safer not to mention the fact that Joseph had his own TV in his bedroom, so they didn't have to creep anywhere to watch it.

'Besides, I hardly ever watch TV in the summer holidays. I'd much rather be out cycling. I could be doing that now,' he said hopefully. 'I need some fresh air.'

'I told you Tim, no cycling today. We've got to go down to the police station now. Go and put on a clean shirt and brush your hair. Then, when I get home from work this evening we need to talk some more about that tutor I told you about. The summer holidays will be a good time for you to catch up with your reading.'

CHAPTER THREE

AT THE POLICE STATION

Tim looked around quickly to make sure there was nobody in the street whom he knew, particularly none of his friends. This was *so* embarrassing. Mum had his hand in a vice-like grip and was hauling him towards the car as if he was four like Frannie. As if she thought he was going to make a break for it and run off. What was the point? Where could he go?

Unfortunately the car was parked a little way down the street and several neighbours tut-tutted at him over their garden walls as they passed. It seemed that everyone had seen the police cars. They all knew he was in trouble. No wonder Mum was in such a state. She dropped his hand to fumble with her car keys.

Tim turned away from the old couple moaning to each other about him over the wall. He stood facing his own house and that of Mr Wizer next door. A flick of movement at an upstairs window caught his eye. It was Mr Wizer. He drew the curtain and glared down at Tim, holding his gaze with an evil stare from his piercing black eyes. The sinister scar above his left eyebrow made Tim think of knife fights and violent brawls. He felt like a snake being charmed by a snake charmer. He wanted desperately to look away, but he couldn't. His body prickled all over. Mr Wizer raised a clenched fist and shook it at Tim. Then, abruptly, he pulled the curtain shut. Tim knew then that Mr Wizer was going to get him, somehow or other.

'Get in the car, Tim! I haven't got all day!'

He was trembling all over as he threw himself into the seat beside Mum. She noticed, of course, and suddenly the anger seemed to flow out of her like air from a deflated balloon. She wasn't mad about the neighbours knowing about him any more, just sad.

'Don't be frightened about this trip to the police station, Timmy. They only want to give you a good talking to. They want to make sure you understand the consequences of what you've done. But they aren't going to *do* anything to you.'

But Tim was still imagining just what Mr Wizer might do to him. He could only mutter '*Please* don't call me Timmy, Mum! It sounds so soppy! I'm eleven now, remember.'

That made Mum cross all over again. They drove through town in complete silence. Tim wanted to say he was sorry, but he just couldn't. In lots of ways he wasn't really sorry at all. Oh yes, he was sorry he'd disturbed Mum's night by phoning the police. He was sorry they'd accused her of making the hoax call because he'd used her name.

But he *wasn't* sorry he'd phoned. He remembered how he felt when he thought he might be too late. When he thought it might be *his* fault if the police didn't get there in time. What if he hadn't called at all and there really *had* been a murder? What about that? Why didn't people concentrate on his good intentions instead of going on about his understandable mistakes?

They had to wait for ages in the police station, even though they had an appointment. Mum got more and more edgy and restless. Tim kept quiet. It was the only thing he could do. Eventually he was called into the sergeant's office, all by himself. He felt very small and guilty as he stood in front of the large policeman.

'So, err . . . Timothy, exactly what sort of skulduggery do you think your neighbour is up to?' said the sergeant at last.

'Skul . . . skul what?' stammered Tim.

'Skulduggery. Underhand practices, trickery, wickedness. Just what particular brand of skulduggery is he up to—in your opinion?'

The sergeant rocked back in his chair and regarded Tim with steely eyes. Tim gulped. Skulduggery indeed.

He'd never even heard of it. He couldn't decide if the policeman was serious or just taking the mickey. Should he tell him what he really feared about Mr Wizer or was he just trying to trap him?

A sudden slight twitch of the man's lips decided him. If he said what he really thought about Mr Wizer then they'd go on at him again about unfounded accusations. After a third time he might really be in trouble. He wasn't going to risk it.

'Nothing, sir. He doesn't appear to have done anything. It was just a mistake. I thought the video was real. I thought he was murdering someone! I'm sorry, sir. I was just trying to be a . . . a good citizen, sir.'

There. Was that good enough? Was that the sort of thing they wanted to hear? Tim breathed a sigh of relief as the policeman started telling him off, just as Mum had said they would. He'd obviously got it about right. He listened solemnly to all the policeman's stern warnings, nodding enthusiastically and saying 'Yes, sir!' in what he thought

were the right places.

But he wasn't really listening. Not with his whole self, just enough to look and sound right. Inside he was wondering what Mr Wizer was going to do to get back at him and how he was going to defend himself.

At last it was over, and Mum was called in.

'I've instructed your son to write a formal letter of apology to Mr Wizer,' said the sergeant, 'I hope you will ensure that he delivers it personally.'

'Certainly, sergeant. I'll make sure he writes a sincere letter to Mr Wizer. And I assure you that Tim will *never* do anything like this again.'

Tim knew that people of his age didn't get sent to jail. But he still breathed a sigh of relief as they left the police station at last. The car was stifling and the seat as hot as a patch of desert sand. In his relief at being free he forgot Mum's earlier threats of jobs to be done and being grounded.

'Can I go swimming this afternoon, Mum? It's so hot!'

His mother's expression refreshed

his memory.

'I mean, can I take Frannie swimming? She'd love it, and I'd make sure to keep her armbands on. It would give Mrs Trump a good rest too. You know how she always wilts in this weather.'

Mrs Trump was their child-minder. She came in every day to look after Frannie while Mum was at work. She was meant to look after both of them really, but she was so old and doddery that Tim always felt *he* was looking after her.

'You've *got* to settle down and write this letter, Tim. It's important that Mr Wizer gets it as soon as possible.'

'Can't I do the letter when you get home tonight? You *know* I'll never be able to do it by myself!' said Tim bitterly.

But Tim knew that a letter of apology would not save him from Mr Wizer's clutches, no matter how well it was composed or spelt. What if he planned to get his own back today, while Mum was at work? He lived right next door. He could get at Tim in seconds. Frannie was hardly more than a baby and Mrs Trump would be about as much use as a chocolate teapot when it came to defending him. What was he going to do?

CHAPTER FOUR

TIM'S TUTOR

It was most unlike Mum to expect him to write a letter like that without any help. She was the one who had supported him all his school life. The one who had argued with the teachers that he wasn't 'backward' as they thought, or 'thick' as the other kids labelled him at first. She was the one who had fought for special lessons for Tim to help him learn to read and spell like everyone else.

Tim was a whizz at maths, especially problems he could do in his head. He was good at science and art and technology. He knew masses about geography and history and environmental issues. He just had difficulty reading about them, or writing down what he knew. He had a form of word blindness. Reading was like a secret code he was always just on the verge of cracking, but he couldn't quite get it.

'Oh dear, you're right of course. But I must get to work. And I'll have to stay on late to make up for taking time off to go to the police station. So there won't be time to do it tonight. I wonder if Rhonda could come tomorrow instead of next week? Then she could start by helping you with the letter.'

Tim groaned. He'd known about the tutor that Mum and Dad had planned for him for ages. They were worried about him going to secondary school. His headmaster had suggested that he stayed on another year at primary school. His birthday was in July, so he would be just a month older than some of the children a year below him.

But Mum and Dad realised how awful it would be for him to leave his friends behind. They knew he would feel that he had failed somehow if he had to repeat Year Six. Dad had suggested the tutor instead. Tim had been so anxious not to be left behind that he would have agreed to anything. But now the time had come he knew he didn't want to spend his summer studying. He had to investigate Mr Wizer. He had to find Minty.

'I'll go round and see Rhonda on the way to work and ask her. I don't suppose she'll mind,' said Mum.

Rhonda. A lot of Mum's friends were teachers, but he couldn't remember any of them being called Rhonda. Was she the one with the huge false teeth? Or the young blonde one that played the flute at concerts Tim was sometimes dragged unwillingly to? No, surely she was called Rhoda—or maybe Rhona. And the one with the teeth was Rose.

The only person *he* knew called Rhonda was a really tall, skinny, red-haired girl that the boys had all called 'Giraffe'. They weren't very original, the boys in his school. She was a real boffin. Always top in every subject. Even though she was a couple of years older and had left their school ages ago people still talked about her. 'Rhonda the Giraffe—the walking, talking dictionary.'

That Rhonda was just the sort of person who would end up some poor boy's tutor in the summer holidays, when she was grown up. She'd probably enjoy it. He happened to see her quite often because their child-minder, Mrs Trump, was her grandmother. Rhonda went to the library after school every day to do her homework, then came and waited outside his house for Mrs Trump to finish at 5.30 p.m. before they walked home together.

Mum had once suggested asking her in every day while she waited for her grandmother. Tim was aghast! Even when Rhonda was in his school he had hardly ever even spoken to her. She was from a different planet. An alien. A girl.

'Rhonda who?' he asked softly, not

liking the horrid churning feeling he was beginning to get in the pit of his stomach.

'Rhonda Trump, of course! How many Rhondas do we know?'

'But Rhonda *can't* be a tutor! She can't be *my* tutor! She's just a girl!'

'I know Rhonda's only thirteen, but she's very bright. She'd make a good tutor. You know I only want what's best for you, Tim.'

'No you don't!' said Tim furiously. 'You want to punish me by telling that toffee-nosed Rhonda I can't read properly. She'll just make fun of me. I won't have her! She'll cross the threshold of my room over my dead body! And that may be sooner than you think! That Mr Wizer's out to get me too, you know. He's plotting some horrible way to murder me, right at this very second. You'll all be sorry when he succeeds!'

Mum sighed. 'You really have become obsessed with that man, haven't you? Well, the sooner you forget him, the better it will be for you. He is *not* out to get you. Nor am I and nor is Rhonda. I think she's very nice. Her grandmother asked if there was anything she could do during the summer to make a little extra money—housework, I think she meant. You know they are very hard-up since her father lost his job. I *do* want to help out, but I really think she's too young to spend the summer cleaning other people's houses! Working with you for a few hours every day will be much nicer for her, I'm sure. That way you and I can be helping her too. It's about time you thought of someone else for a change, Tim. And there's no reason for her to go into your room. I know how you feel about that. She can work with you in the dining room every day. There will be lots of room at the big table for all your books.'

Tim sulked for the rest of the way home but it made no difference. Mum was not going to change her mind. Rhonda was going to be his tutor and that was that. As soon as he got home he went into Dad's study and sat in his chair. He longed to hear his Dad's voice, to feel his soft beard against his cheek as he gave him the dreaded tickle treatment. If *Dad* told him that Mr Wizer wasn't out to get him, he would believe it. But Dad was over eight thousand miles away.

Tim was aware of someone moving in the next door garden. He leant quietly over the desk and moved the curtain aside so he could see better. It was Mr Wizer—he might have known. But Tim had never seen him take an interest in gardening before, so what was he up to? He was shovelling furiously in the hard, summer-baked earth. He was obviously going to bury something. Jumping jellyfish! Was it a stash of notes from a bank raid? A body? Something even more evil and grisly? Tim's mind was racing with the possibilities.

He jumped as Mum came through the door. He quickly dropped the curtain and sank back into Dad's chair.

'Remember I said I'll be late home tonight because of having to make up time? So you help Mrs Trump get Frannie to bed tonight. OK?'

She kissed the top of his head. Tim

sighed. He *always* put Frannie to bed when Mum was late home. Mrs Trump hated to climb the stairs and Frannie always liked to have her story and songs in bed. But he said nothing. It wasn't Mrs Trump's fault she was an old lady any more than it was his fault he was dyslexic and couldn't read well yet.

He sat back in the big chair and imagined what a real detective would do. He would undertake surveillance, like the detectives on TV. He would watch every move Mr Wizer made. He would take note of when he went out and when he came in. Of what he was carrying and what he wore. They would all be important clues to what Mr Wizer was really up to. What was that word the policeman had used? Skulduggery! Yes, that was it. Underhand practices, trickery and wickedness, he had said it meant.

Tim thought of that sinister scar and those evil-looking eyes almost hypnotising him. Mr Wizer was up to some sort of skulduggery and it was up to Tim to see that he didn't get away with it.

CHAPTER FIVE

RHONDA

Tim lingered over his breakfast. He didn't have even one more day of freedom to look forward to. Rhonda was coming for lunch every day, then she was going to spend two hours reading, writing and spelling with Tim. The first thing on the agenda was the letter.

Tim spent the morning in his bedroom, ignoring Frannie's pleas to come down and play with her. His room was a loft conversion and it had a special staircase that folded back into the room when the stairs weren't in use. Although he wasn't meant to, Tim had worked out how he could pull it up after him when he wanted to make sure no one would bother him.

Frannie was the only one in the family who ever made it up the stairs, apart from Mavis, the cleaning lady, who cleaned Tim's room thoroughly once a month. In between he was supposed to keep it clean and tidy himself. Dad had always respected his desire for a private place and would never come up without being invited. And Mum would never come up at all because of Tim's pets. Not only did Mum hate little furry animals, but she was allergic to them too.

Tim had three gerbils, two hamsters, a rat and a plastic tank full of stick insects. Now stick insects aren't the least furry, but for some reason Mum hated the stick insects even more than the rodents. And that was when she thought he only had two of them. The stick insects had been doing rather a lot of multiplying recently and were threatening to overflow the tank.

Tim thought about Dad as he refilled his pets' food bowls and made sure the stick insects had enough leaves. Dad was a scientist and he had always taught Tim that to find something out you must be logical. You must never make wild guesses. You must look at all the evidence, then draw your conclusions from that. Then when you had what you thought was a conclusion, you must test it to find out if it was true.

Tim took out a big piece of paper. First he drew a picture of Mr Wizer's nasty, sneering face. Tim was good at drawing and the face was so lifelike it actually made him shudder. That was to show how much Mr Wizer seemed to hate him, for no really good reason.

Then he drew a picture of Minty, with a big red line across her. Minty had disappeared. There was still no trace of her.

Next he drew the fire in the back garden. Why had Mr Wizer been burning stuff? What was the real reason? What else had he been about to burn?

Then there was Mr Wizer's threatening gesture as Tim got into the car yesterday. Tim was certain he meant to do him harm.

The last clue was Mr Wizer digging in the garden. He certainly wasn't planting vegetables. What had he been burying? Was it something he didn't have time to burn? Tim considered his page of clues. It was certainly suspicious behaviour, but as yet there was no explanation for it. Burning, burying—perhaps he was destroying evidence of some sort. Criminals always tried to destroy the evidence. But how could he prove it?

Rhonda arrived for lunch complete with her battered school lunch-box. Mrs Trump was as surprised as Tim.

'You don't need that, girl,' she said. 'You know Mrs Randolph said she'd give you your dinner when you were here. Look, she's got in these big pizzas for you all. I told her they were your favourite.'

'I've come here to work, Gran. I'm not a charity case.'

'All the more for us then,' said Tim airily.

Frannie didn't want much, as usual. But although he worked his way steadily through the two big pizzas Tim couldn't help watching Rhonda cheerfully eat her two small, thin peanut butter sandwiches. For some reason the pizza didn't taste nearly as good as it usually did. Once Rhonda looked up and caught him watching her.

'You'll *know* me next time, won't you, Timmy?' she said pointedly.

'This is *my* kitchen,' he said defensively. 'I can look anywhere I like in my own kitchen, can't I? And my name's *not* Timmy!'

'That's a coincidence. *My* name's not "Giraffe"!' Shutting her lunch-box with a bang, she walked out of the kitchen. First round to Rhonda.

Tim hadn't realised she actually *knew* they called her 'Giraffe'. It wasn't as if they yelled it at her or anything. He wondered how she knew.

He spent the next half hour being as nice as possible to Frannie, to put off having to start work with Rhonda. He let her sit on his beanbag with him while she watched *Sesame Street* on TV.

'This is exactly the same as when I was four,' he told a delighted Frannie. 'Big Bird hasn't changed a bit.'

But when the programme finished, Mrs Trump came in and turned the TV off. She took Frannie into the kitchen to make cupcakes for tea, and Tim knew he couldn't put off the dreaded moment any longer. He sidled into the dining room and sat down as far as possible from Rhonda.

She was deep in a book and didn't even notice him for a few minutes. Eventually a big yawn escaped him. Rhonda looked up, obviously as displeased to see him as he was to see her. But she came over immediately and slid a pad of paper towards him.

'Your mother said you had to write a letter. Here's the pad. You tell me what you want to say and I'll tell you how to spell it.'

'Jumping jellyfish! Who says I need to know how to spell stuff?' he said aggressively, as if that wasn't exactly why she was there.

'Jellyfish don't jump, Tim. They

undulate. Do you know that means they move about with a wavy motion?'

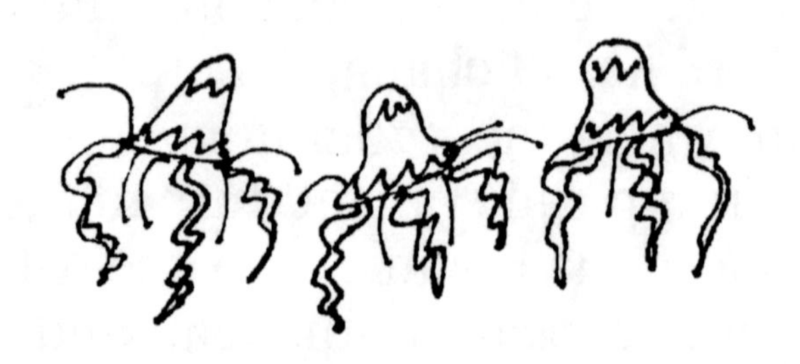

Tim threw the pad down on the table. 'I know exactly how jellyfish move. Do *you* know that you could eat your own stupid words—if I was to stuff a dictionary down your throat!'

Rhonda ignored that. 'I'm sure you know lots more than me about natural history, Tim. But I know you have a specific learning difficulty. I've read up about it and I know that being unable to spell is a part of it. You have that in common with many great people in history—Einstein, Winston Churchill, Hans Christian Andersen, Susan Hampshire.'

She sounds just like a teacher, thought Tim. But he was interested, in spite of himself. 'Who's Susan Hampshire?'

He held his own at school by being good at so many other things, but he had never heard anyone consider his problem in a positive light before.

'She's a very famous actress and she also writes books about dyslexia. I know you don't want me to be here any more than I want to spend my summer teaching a . . . a boy. Any sort of boy. So why don't we both just get on with it and get it over with as soon as possible?'

Tim realised that she'd not called him a *stupid* boy simply so she wouldn't hurt his feelings. She could have called him anything. But she hadn't. Maybe she wasn't going to be as bad as he'd thought. Silently, he picked up the biro and put his address at the top of the page. His mother had spent many hours teaching him to spell his address. Then he looked up expectantly.

'What do you want to say?' Rhonda prompted.

'*I* don't want to say anything. It's Mum and the police who are making me write this letter,' he said crossly.

'Tell me exactly what happened,' she

ordered, carefully putting a marker into her book and giving him her full attention.

To his own astonishment, Tim told her everything, even about Minty and the terrifying fire in the garden.

When he had finished, Rhonda said, 'Perhaps we should just put a letter bomb into the envelope.'

Tim's eyes opened wide.

'Only joking,' she assured him. 'You really are gullible, Tim. That means you'll believe anything,' she added. 'Still, I do think you did the right thing, phoning the police. It's always better to be safe than sorry. It's only because you did it before, over the cat business, that they think you're trying it on. They think you've got a vendetta against this guy. He sounds to me like he's got one against you!'

'A . . . what?' asked Tim. Jumping jellyfish! No wonder they called her a walking dictionary.

She wrote the word on a piece of paper.

' "Vendetta". It's a feud,' she said, 'a war between people, rather than countries. But there's no reason why *we* shouldn't have one too.'

These words made Tim feel better. Rhonda was on his side. He wasn't alone against Mr Wizer, after all. With his logical detecting skills and Rhonda's brain power, they could outwit his evil neighbour together.

CHAPTER SIX

INVESTIGATION

They both agreed that it would be better in the long run to write a proper letter of apology that even Tim's mother couldn't complain about. Rhonda composed it, using so many long words and complicated phrases that Tim hardly understood any of it anyway. It didn't feel like anything he would ever say, so he was quite happy to sign the bottom and forget about it. By the time they'd finished talking, written the letter and Tim had slowly copied it out, the two hours were over.

By then Tim was itching to get out and start investigating. He needed to know so much more about Mr Wizer. But that was going to be difficult while he was grounded. What he really needed was to follow Mr Wizer when he left the house, and find out where he went, what he did and who he met.

For a moment he thought of asking Rhonda to help. She was obviously really interested in the situation. But then he remembered how he'd promised himself not to co-operate with Rhonda. At first he had been relieved that she was on his side, but thinking about the conversation, hadn't it been a bit much when she'd said '*We* could have our own vendetta.' She'd come to help him with his spelling, for heaven's sake!

Mr Wizer was *his* neighbour. Tim was the one who'd been threatened, who'd had to phone the police twice already. Who invited her to take over his investigation anyway? And that's what she would do, too. She thought she knew everything about everything. She would take over completely and he would be left looking silly. No, he might not be able to spell all those detective words, but he knew he would be better off sleuthing alone.

Tim said a short goodbye to Rhonda and bounded up the stairs to Dad's study. There were signs of more digging in next door's garden. A pot plant had been shoved unevenly into the top of the freshly dug mound, probably to make it look as if the digging had been for planting. But Mr Wizer obviously knew absolutely nothing about gardening. Not only did it look like the sort of plant that should live indoors but he hadn't even bothered to take it out of its pot before he'd thrust it into the earth.

Tim felt this confirmed that the digging had more to do with Mr Wizer's skulduggery than with any sort of horticulture. 'Horticulture', the art of gardening. Tim knew a lot of long words too, even if he couldn't spell them. Maybe he didn't need Rhonda after all, although it still felt good to know she was on his side.

He decided to take his investigations further by chatting up Mrs Trump. She loved to gossip, and had spent most weekdays for the last four years or so eagerly watching the goings-on in

Gladstone Place. Hopefully Rhonda would have reported that the tutoring had gone well, so she ought to be in a good mood.

His hunch was right. Obviously both Mum and Mrs Trump had feared that he and Rhonda might clash, so the child-minder was all smiles when he appeared. He was relieved to see that Rhonda had gone, which left the field wide open for his investigations.

Mrs Trump poured him a glass of juice and Frannie proudly presented him with a sticky cupcake, fresh from the oven. Things were definitely looking up. As guardedly as he could, Tim quizzed the old lady about the comings and goings of Mr Wizer.

He soon found out that Mr Wizer worked odd hours, down at the dockyard. That didn't help Tim very much. Half the people in Plymouth worked in the dockyard, as anything from secretaries to labourers. Lots of people were on flexitime. But Mrs Trump had noticed that he had some regular shifts, on Tuesdays, Fridays and Saturdays, starting mid-morning.

'He's never out for very long though,' she mused thoughtfully. 'As if he had to rush home to feed the dog, or something. But he doesn't have a dog—not that I've ever seen, anyway.'

Tim thought it seemed unlikely for Mr Wizer to have any sort of pet, unless it was something like a boa constrictor or a poisonous tarantula. He knew you didn't have to feed reptiles or spiders very often. Another puzzling clue. But tomorrow was Friday. It would be a good time to investigate the mound in the garden.

Next morning Tim cleared the breakfast things while Mum was getting ready for work. He watched her out of the corner of his eye as he did so. The sooner he convinced her that he was behaving sensibly, the sooner he'd be allowed out of the house. She was obviously impressed, but he knew he must be careful.

He gave a huge yawn. She immediately bustled over and ruffled his hair.

'You sound tired, dear. Aren't you sleeping well in this heat?'

'I'm sleeping fine, Mum. It's just . . . well it's so stuffy being indoors all the time. I suppose I'm not getting enough fresh air.'

'Of course you must have fresh air, Tim. I never meant you had to actually stay in the house every moment of the day. Why don't you spend the morning playing in the garden?'

Yes! It was as simple as that. He'd

scored. Now he could go and dig up Mr Wizer's patch and see what he'd buried.

'It's so hot you can get out the paddling pool for Frannie. She'd love that, and I'm sure Mrs Trump would be grateful too. The heat's too much for her outdoors. But it will be easy for you to watch Frannie if you're outside anyway.'

Jumping jellyfish! How could he possibly nip over the wall and dig in next door's garden with Frannie hot on his heels?

'Errr . . . I'm not sure about that, Mum. Isn't it too dangerous now, what with global warming and everything? Frannie might get skin cancer if she goes in the paddling pool in the middle of summer. Wouldn't she be better indoors with Mrs Trump, watching her videos?'

'Just make sure she's got her little sunhat on, and a long-sleeved T-shirt, and I'm sure she'll be fine. You could even put up the parasol over the pool if you're really worried.'

Foiled again!

At 10 o'clock Tim hid in the long velvet folds of the living room curtains. Here he had a good view of the road in front of the house but he couldn't be seen. Except by Frannie, of course. She found him within minutes.

'Are you playing hide-and-seek, Tim? Can I play too?'

Tim knew that if he refused she would probably go wailing to Mrs Trump. Now Mrs Trump might be old and doddery but she still had all her marbles. It might seem quite normal to a four year old for Tim to be hiding in the curtains, but Mrs Trump wouldn't be so easily fooled. She'd want to know what was going on.

'It's not hide and seek, Frannie, it's sardines. But it's a very boring game and I'm sure you wouldn't like it.'

'I would, Tim, really I would,' clamoured Frannie.

'All right then, but you have to stop yelling. One of the most important bits of this game is that you have to stand in silence inside the curtain for a long time, just like a sardine in a tin. Now I'm big, so I can do it for ages. But you're so little you won't be able to do it for long. So just wrap yourself in your curtain and stay quiet as a mouse. Then creep out and play with Mrs Trump. I will stay still and quiet for as long as I can, then I'll come and tell you how how many minutes it was. Then next time you can see if you can do it for longer.'

Frannie managed to remain sardined inside the curtain for at least ten minutes before she wandered off, but it was a good half hour before Tim saw Mr Wizer emerge from the front door of number 30. With a sigh of relief Tim saw him get into his car and drive away. Surely he was safe for a few hours at least.

As Tim dragged out the plastic pool and started filling it up with the hose, he tried to decide how to distract Frannie while he investigated the garden next door. He was perched in the fork of the small apple tree, looking longingly at the pile of disturbed earth when Frannie climbed up beside him. They looked at the pile in silence for a few moments.

'He's not as good a digger as Daddy, is he Tim?' asked Frannie thoughtfully.

Tim had a brainwave. 'Do you think I should just nip over and dig it up a bit better for him? But we won't hurt his feelings by telling him *I* did it. We'll just let him think that was how he left it. He probably wouldn't notice the difference as he's not such a good gardener. In fact, we won't tell anyone about it, not Mum or Mrs Trump, in case they tell him. That would be a good plan, wouldn't it, Frannie? You could be my partner. Your most important job would be to keep the secret. What do you think?'

'Can I dig too, Tim? I'm a good digger!'

'But Frannie, I need someone to hold the hose for filling the pool. That's a much more important job.'

Frannie eagerly took over the job of

pool filler. Relieved, Tim grabbed a trowel from the shed and climbed over the wall. Luckily, Mr Wizer's house was at the end of the terrace, so his garden was only overlooked by Tim's house. Tim cautiously removed the potted plant and started to dig.

He had to move a lot of earth before he found what he was looking for. The shape and colour were unmistakable. It was a furry black cat.

CHAPTER SEVEN

BLACK CAT, WHITE FACE

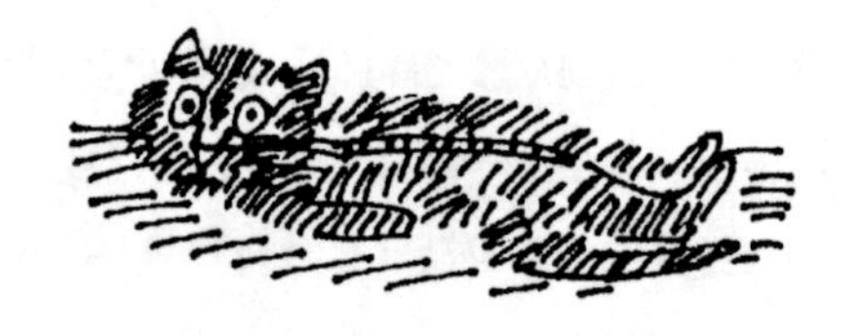

Tim's heart skipped a beat and he felt as if he was going to throw up. Then he touched the fur, matted and encrusted with earth. He knew at once that it wasn't Minty. He turned the body over with his trowel. It was light and flimsy. There seemed to be nothing to it. He wiped the head on his shorts. The big green eyes that stared up at him were nothing but glass.

He picked the thing up and shook the earth from it. It was a toy. He looked closer and found a zipper, clogged up with fresh earth. No, not a toy, a pyjama case. Frannie had one like it, but hers was a blue pony. He carefully tried to unzip the case, struggling with the stiff zip. He could only get it open a short way so he pushed his fingers inside it, fumbling for the contents he was sure he could feel.

His thrusting fingers found and grasped a piece of cloth. He pulled it as far through the hole as he could get it. Tim's mouth dropped open in amazement. It was soft, pale blue material, with pink elephants gambolling about all over it. It looked like a pair of child's pyjamas.

Tim quickly filled up the hole and patted down the earth, trying to make it look just as it had before he started to dig. He plonked the pot plant back on top of the mound and ran for the fence, the black cat clutched under his arm.

He didn't think this was stealing. He was a detective and this was evidence. He scrambled over the wall and stuffed the pyjama case behind the compost heap. Frannie mustn't see it. As he straightened up he heard a sound from next door. Jumping jellyfish! Had Mr

Wizer come back already and spotted what he'd done?

He climbed into the fork of the tree once more and cautiously looked over. In his haste to get away he hadn't been careful with the plant and it had tumbled out of its pot and lay in a crumpled heap on the ground. He had gone over the wall earlier with hardly a care in the world, eager for the opportunity to gather more evidence. But now he'd actually found it, Tim was petrified. He was scared stiff and certainly didn't want to go back.

He looked over his shoulder. The paddling pool was already overflowing and Frannie was now watering her trainers and socks as well as most of the garden. He would have to be quick. He was over the wall in one leap, his heart pounding like an express train. He righted the plant and put it back in its pot. Once he'd brushed the earth out of the petals it didn't look too bad. Perhaps he'd never notice. As he pushed the plant into the mound with a last firm shove, he looked up at Mr Wizer's window. Surely that was a movement behind the curtain?

He dived quickly behind a bush. Perhaps he'd been mistaken. Perhaps the movement had been from his own house. But Mrs Trump never climbed the stairs. She couldn't be up there. No, the movement had definitely come from Mr Wizer's house. The ground floor flat, always let to students, was empty for the summer holidays. He had definitely seen the swish of a curtain at the upstairs window. Mr Wizer's window. Tim peered carefully over the top of the bush. At the bottom of the window he saw the shape of a white face.

He hardly knew how he got back over the wall. He grabbed Frannie by the hand and dragged her back into the house, muttering something about juice and biscuits. It wasn't till much later that he realised he'd left the hose turned on. It would be just his luck if some nosy neighbour phoned the water board and complained about them. There wasn't a hosepipe ban yet, but some people did get very heated about wasted water. He could be grounded for life.

Mrs Trump shooed them back out into the garden eventually. While Frannie frolicked in the paddling pool, Tim settled himself in the branches of a tree, well concealed by leaves from all but Frannie.

He thought long and hard about what he had discovered. The whole thing was what Dad would call a conundrum, or . . . there was another word but he couldn't think of it. The whole thing *was* a mystery to him.

Why had Mr Wizer buried a child's pyjama case in the garden? Obviously to conceal it. But who was he hiding it from? The police? It must be vital evidence that he had to hide so it couldn't lead the police to him. And why did the black cat case look so much like Minty? Minty had disappeared. The pretend cat had appeared, only to be hidden. Tim couldn't make sense of it. He needed more clues, more evidence.

He hardly dared think about the face at the window. It couldn't be Mr Wizer. Surely if it was and he'd come home early he'd be over here already, eager to complain to Mum about Tim wrecking his garden.

After lunch he went up to Dad's study to think in peace. Whose was the face? Had it seen him? He was sure that it must have done, drawn to the window by movements in the garden, just as he had been by Mr Wizer digging.

As he sat and stewed, the words of a song were going through his brain, over and over again. It was all about the friendly neighbours you meet on *Sesame Street.* He'd heard it hundreds of times when he was little. Now it was one of Frannie's favourites.

It was really annoying him now. Jumping jellyfish! He was trying to concentrate here on what might be a matter of life or death—his, and Frannie had the TV blaring away. He stormed out of the study and yelled down the stairs.

'Can't you turn that awful racket *down,* Frannie! I'm trying to work up here!'

Rhonda's head came round the living room door followed by a bemused looking Frannie. 'What on earth are you yelling about, Tim?' said Rhonda. 'We aren't even *watching* TV. We're playing "Tummy Ache".'

Tim's legs felt leaden as he walked slowly downstairs and into the living room. Sure enough, the TV screen was blank. The floor was covered with bits of Frannie's favourite board game. Without a word he went back upstairs.

As he closed the study door he could still hear it. They were on to counting now. He remembered it well.

'One, two, three, four, five, six, seven, eight, *nine,* ten.'

Could it be coming from the house on the other side, number 26? Very unlikely. It was one of the few houses like theirs in the street which still belonged to one family. Most of them had been divided up into flats. An elderly couple lived at number 26. Although they had many grandchildren—he had often been shown their photos—they all lived in Australia and had never been to

Plymouth. Besides, he knew they only had one TV, and that was down in their living room.

Anyway, number 26 was on the other side of Frannie's and Mum's bedrooms. You could never hear a TV through that many walls. The study and the bathroom were on the right as you went up the stairs. Mr Wizer's house was the only one on the right, and his flat was on the other side of the wall. It had to be coming from there. Had Mr Wizer left it on just to annoy him?

Tim went into the bathroom and got his tooth-glass from the shelf. He pressed it to the wall, where he had originally heard the screams in the night, but could hear nothing. Perhaps Mr Wizer had two TVs, so he could watch in bed.

Tim thought about the layout of the houses. Frannie's bedroom, the one in the front, was much smaller than Mum and Dad's. If Mr Wizer had that one for his bedroom, then the bigger room would be the living room. That seemed logical. The bathroom and the study would be on the side farthest from Tim. Only in Mr Wizer's house, the study would be the kitchen.

Tim took the glass back into the study and put it against what he thought must be Mr Wizer's living room wall. The sounds of 'It's alright to cry' came through loud and clear.

'What are you doing, Tim?' asked Rhonda curiously, from the open doorway.

'None of your business!' he replied crossly, putting down the glass and running downstairs.

It was a very distracted Tim that Rhonda had to cope with that afternoon. She wisely made no comment on what he had been doing in the study. But they didn't get very far with his spellings. Just at that moment Tim doubted if he could even spell his own name.

'Why don't we do some reading

instead?' suggested Rhonda, after an unsuccessful half hour. 'Why don't you go and get whatever book you're interested in, and we'll read that.'

'The sort of books I'm interested in are *not* the sort of books they give me to read!' he replied crossly.

'Well, there's not much point to that!' she said. 'Why would anyone want to read something that's boring? You just get whatever you want and we'll read it together.'

'You mean you'll read it to me?' he asked hopefully. That way he could get on with trying to sort out the conundrum while she droned on with the book.

'No, we'll read it together. It's called paired reading. We're partners. I read all of it, and you read at exactly the same time, but obviously you only read the words you know. That way you still get the practice, but it's not dead slow, like when you're reading it to someone.'

Tim went and got the book Dad had been reading to him just before he left. It was the *Complete Works of Sherlock*

Holmes. The famous Victorian detective was one of Tim's favourites. Maybe he could get some ideas from it. They read together for the rest of the time and Tim found it went better than any reading he'd ever done before. He got over the embarrassment of them both reading in unison and was soon deep in the story.

Just before Rhonda left he asked her 'What's another name for a conundrum or a riddle?'

'Perhaps you're thinking of enigma,' she said helpfully.

I wish Sherlock Holmes was here, thought Tim. I'm sure it would be a good case for him, 'The Black Cat and White Face Enigma.'

CHAPTER EIGHT

REAL EVIDENCE

As soon as Rhonda had gone Tim raced up the stairs and into Dad's study. He picked up the glass from the desk and pressed it against the wall. Nothing. He could hear nothing at all. Feeling highly frustrated he threw himself down in Dad's chair and sighed deeply.

If only Dad was here. He was sure Dad would listen to him. Dad would help him solve this problem. Tim conjured up the figure of his father in his mind. Tall, like Tim. Lots of hair and beard. Mum liked his beard short but Tim and Frannie preferred it when he'd been away for a long time and hadn't trimmed it. Then it was full and soft and fluffy, rather like a pet animal. Perhaps that's why Mum didn't like it that way. She hated furry things.

The reassuring image of Dad in his mind calmed Tim's racing thoughts. Then he tried to imagine Dad talking to him, giving advice on how to succeed. For he never told him the answer to conundrums, only how to go about working them out for himself. 'Look at the evidence,' was what he seemed to be saying.

Tim pulled the evidence sheet towards him. He added the black cat pyjama case, and the white face at the window. Then he drew the wall between the study and Mr Wizer's flat, with himself on one side and a TV showing Big Bird on the other. That was obviously *Sesame Street.*

Evidence! Jumping jellyfish! He had a real piece of evidence and he hadn't even examined it properly yet. He raced downstairs and out into the back garden, pausing only to pick up an empty carrier bag from the kitchen. He rescued the dirty black cat case from behind the compost heap and hid it carefully in the bag. Then he ran back upstairs. This time he went right up to his own room and pulled the staircase up after him.

The cat looked limp and pathetic as it lay on Tim's floor, its green eyes staring sightlessly. Tim got his hairbrush and gave the cat a thorough brushing, releasing loads of fresh earth onto the carpet. Then he worked on the zip, running a big pencil up and down over the teeth. Mum always did that when his anorak zip stuck.

After a few minutes' struggle he managed to get it to open half-way. He reached in and pulled out the blue elephant pyjamas. Tim laid them out on the floor. He let down the staircase and crept down into Frannie's room. She had ears like a bat and he certainly didn't want her to butt in at the moment. He rummaged in her cupboard until he found what he wanted, then ran back upstairs.

He laid Frannie's pyjamas down on the floor beside the ones from the black cat. Frannie's were slightly bigger. Frannie was four but quite tall for her age, like Tim. The owner of the pyjamas must be about her age, three or four years old. Who owned the elephant pyjamas? Frannie's were blue too, so that was no clue. But he had a strong feeling that the pyjamas and the black cat had belonged to a little boy.

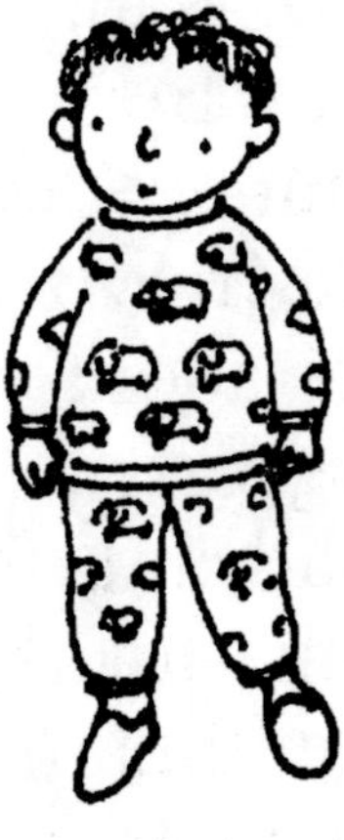

Tim pushed the black cat and both pairs of pyjamas under his bed. He went back down to the study, an idea brewing in his mind. He drew the big piece of paper showing his evidence towards him. The last picture, of the white face at the window, stared up at him. He remembered Mr Wizer's threatening gesture towards him. His body had seemed to fill up the whole window.

In his picture the white face was small, right down at the bottom of the window. When he'd seen it, the face had flashed away too quickly for him to recognise it. But now he was sure. The white face at the window was the face of a child. A little three or four year old boy who usually wore blue pyjamas with elephants on them.

That was his deduction from the evidence. He knew scientists were always making deductions. They worked things out from the evidence they had. But then they always proved that the deduction was correct. What Tim needed was proof.

Mr Wizer had been living next door for about eight months. He went away regularly, in the same way that Tim's Dad did, for his work. He was usually gone for three or four weeks at a time. He had never had a child with him when he came back. No child or wife or partner had ever been seen in Gladstone Place. Tim had already found that out from Mrs Trump.

Of course, there was no reason he shouldn't have a child there with him, but if he did, then who was he? Who looked after him when he went to work? Even Tim was never allowed to stay at home alone for a whole day when Mum was at work. Surely nobody would leave a little boy like that all alone, even for the short shifts that Mrs Trump had mentioned?

If there was someone else in there looking after the child, why had they never been seen? If the little boy was staying with him, why did he never go out? Little kids were always going out in their pushchairs. They went shopping, and to the park and the library. They went to playgroup and gymtots. They went out with their Mums or minders to friends' houses. Other kids came over to play with them.

If there really *was* a little boy staying next door, why had he never seen little clothes drying in next door's garden? Mr Wizer hung his clothes there. Tim was pretty sure he didn't have a drier, because if it rained, as it often did in Plymouth, then Mr Wizer just left his clothes out until they eventually dried.

The only evidence of the boy's existence was the black cat pyjama case, the tiny blue pyjamas and the face at the window. And of course, the sound of *Sesame Street* coming through the wall. So Tim was sure that there was a little boy next door, but for some reason, Mr Wizer was keeping him hidden. There was only one way to prove his deduction was correct. Tim must somehow get into the flat next door—and look for himself.

He shuddered at the mere thought. Perhaps he should ask Rhonda to help. If Mr Wizer *did* catch him, then at least somebody would know who had done it. Tim swallowed hard. It would be like going into a dragon's lair. But he wasn't St George and he didn't have an enormous spear to defend himself with. He must be mad!

CHAPTER NINE

TRAPDOOR

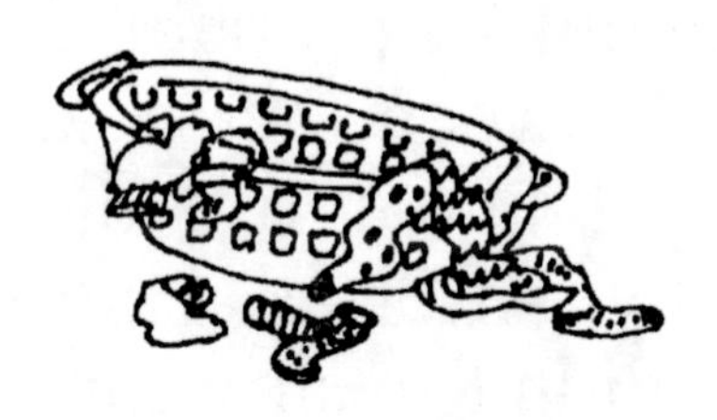

'What are you doing this morning, Mum?' he asked, as casually as possible the next day.

This was one of the two weekends a month that Mum didn't work on a Saturday morning. What Tim had planned might arouse suspicion, so it would be much better for him if the house was empty.

'I expect you'll be taking Frannie out somewhere, won't you, Mum? She's missed you a lot this week, what with no playgroup to keep her busy. She's been *so* looking forward to you taking her out this morning.'

'She didn't mention it,' said Mum.

'She said she wanted to watch *Live and Kicking*. So I thought I'd sort the laundry and put it all away. Mrs Trump does her best, but I can't expect her to know whose socks are which.'

Privately Tim thought that even a monkey could probably tell the difference between the socks of a four year old girl and those of an eleven year old boy. After all, Dad was away, and Mum didn't even wear socks. But he kept his thoughts to himself.

'I'll put the laundry away for you, if you like,' he said cheerfully. 'Frannie really wants to go out. Too much TV is really bad for you, you're always saying so.'

'What are you up to?' asked Mum suspiciously. 'You can't fool me, you know, Tim. You haven't invited Joseph round, have you, so you can smuggle him up to your room and play those awful computer games, hour after hour?'

'Of course not, Mum. I told you that Joseph is spending the summer holidays on his Grandad's farm. I'm not up to anything,' he said, crossing his fingers behind his back.

Mum looked at him with disbelief. He obviously wasn't going to get away with it that easily.

'Well actually there *was* something . . .'

'Well, out with it then. You know you can't keep anything from me.'

Jumping jellyfish! If only you knew! thought Tim.

'I was just going to ask you to get me some new library books. I'm really enjoying reading with Rhonda. Yes, Mum, *really*! But I thought you might be too busy to go into town, just for me. But I thought if you were out with Frannie anyway . . .'

'Oh, Tim! You *know* I'd go and get you books from the library any time you like. I'm *so* pleased you're getting on well with Rhonda. I told you it would all work out well, didn't I, darling!'

'Oh Mum, please!'

Mum laughed and poured herself yet another cup of coffee. Tim breathed a sigh of relief. As the tension relaxed and they sat down together in their usual harmony, Tim began to feel a little guilty. Mum was still looking tired. He was sure she didn't drink so much coffee when Dad was here. For the first time he wondered if she was missing Dad even more than he was. What if he was wrong about the boy hidden away next door? What if he got caught trying to look for him? Mum would go absolutely bananas!

'I'll put the laundry away anyway,' he said helpfully. 'I'll even do some ironing later if you like.'

'Oh Tim, you don't know how to iron! But thanks for offering, anyway.'

'Only 'cos I've never tried it. It doesn't look too difficult to me,' he said as he sidled out of the door with the plastic laundry basket in his arms. Phew! Saved again.

He managed to organise it so he still had Frannie's socks to put away around the time Mr Wizer left for work. Frannie's room overlooked the front garden and he wanted to make absolutely certain Mr Wizer had left, before he made any effort to contact the boy. It would be terrible if, perhaps, Mr Wizer had one Saturday off a month, and Mrs Trump didn't know about it because it was one of the ones she had off herself. Tim had never noticed when Mr Wizer went to work.

He was relieved when Mr Wizer actually got into his car at the usual time and drove away. But the relief evaporated when he found how difficult it was to get Mum and Frannie out of the house. Frannie couldn't leave without watching *Rugrats* and it didn't start until 11 a.m. Mum bustled about doing all sorts of weekend jobs.

'Get me some detective books,' he prompted. 'Any sort will do. Rhonda's got a great method of reading them.'

What if Mr Wizer only worked for half a day on Saturday? Why had he never noticed? What if he'd only gone down to the DIY superstore, like everyone else on a Saturday morning? *Why wouldn't they go!*

But, at last, they did. Tim crept quietly out into the back garden. He might as well try all the obvious methods first.

He climbed over the wall and looked

round cautiously. Nobody was about. The open piece of lawn between the first bush he'd hidden behind and the back door seemed to stretch for miles. Tim took a deep breath.

After all, he *did* have his letter for Mr Wizer in his pocket. Mum seemed to have forgotten he was supposed to deliver it personally, and he certainly wasn't going to volunteer. She seemed to have deliberately tried to forget about Mr Wizer. She hadn't mentioned him once since the trip to the police station.

He would knock on the back door. If there *was* a child in there, and he was *supposed* to be there, then whoever was looking after him would come and answer the door, wouldn't they? He would hand in the letter and ask for it to be given to Mr Wizer. They might think it odd that he was in the *back* garden, but he would just have to risk that.

Tim straightened his shoulders and marched up the garden as if he had every right to be there. He banged hard on the back door, much harder than he had meant to. He took a step back. Jumping jellyfish! What if Mr Wizer was back already? But there was no sound from the house. No footsteps coming down from the flat above. Tim knocked again and waited. No reply. Time for Plan B.

Tim went back indoors. He collected Dad's toolbag from the cupboard under the stairs and went up to his own room at the top of the house. One of the best things about Tim's loft conversion was the huge cupboards on either side of the room. They had sliding doors and were big enough to actually crawl inside and hide things away.

He and Joseph had always thought it was a shame they didn't stretch all round the room. Then they could have had great chasing games in them. But that had been much earlier, just after

Frannie was born. They'd both been very young then. But Tim remembered one important thing about those cupboards. He knew exactly what was behind them.

Against all instructions, Tim had often come up to watch the workmen building his room. He remembered, at the beginning, looking in awe at the long stretch of boarded-over rafters.

'I didn't think our house was so huge up here,' he'd said to Sam, the carpenter.

'It's not all yours, mate!' Sam had said. 'All the houses in this terrace are connected in pairs in their roof spaces. Some of them have been boarded up, but most people don't even realise they could go up into their loft and then down through the trapdoor into next door's house.'

'Really!' said Tim. 'Could I do that?'

'Not for long, mate!' said Sam with a laugh. 'I'm building you a wall.'

But Tim and Joseph had investigated the cupboard space thoroughly. The walls of the cupboards were just thin hardboard, screwed onto a wooden frame.

Tim emptied the cupboard nearest to number 30. He removed the family's suitcases, Minty's padded cat bed, his spare gerbil tanks and his comic collection. He had brought up Dad's best torch, the one on a long stem that you could twist around into any position. He pointed it at the panel opposite the cupboard door and got to work on the screws.

It was harder work than he expected. The screws were in tight. Tim heaved and unscrewed until he was red in the face. But at last he had a panel unfastened. He pushed it aside and shone the torch into the roof space. At the far end he could just make out the outline of the trapdoor that led to Mr Wizer's house.

Tim picked up the torch, crawled through and started slowly across the boarded rafters. He'd just reached the trapdoor when he dimly heard a muffled bang. He stopped and listened. Was that a door banging? Probably, but where? His house—or Mr Wizer's? The next sound gave him the answer.

'Tim! Tim, where *are* you? I forgot to get your library ticket! *Tim!*'

CHAPTER TEN

INVASION OF THE STICK INSECTS

Tim hurtled across the roof space, the noise of his footsteps echoing horribly on the rafter boards. In his haste he fell over his own feet and landed on his face with an awful thud.

'Tim! Whatever are you doing? What's that terrible noise?'

Mum's voice was getting closer. She seemed to be nearly at the top of the main stairs now. Tim scrambled to his feet and dashed across, reaching the hole in his wall at the same moment Mum reached the bottom of his staircase.

'I'm coming up, Tim! I want to know exactly what you're doing up there!'

The folding metal stairs creaked as Mum started to climb. Tim looked around wildly. He could shut the cupboard to conceal the gaping hole in his wall but there were suitcases everywhere. All the stuff from the cupboard was scattered around the room. Mum would want to know why it was out, and insist on him putting it back. Then she would see. Then he would be 'for it'! Grounded until he was eighteen was the least he could expect. All these thoughts flashed through his mind in the split second it took him to glance around.

Oh, why hadn't he pulled the stairs up after him as he usually did? He should have *known* he couldn't depend on the house staying empty for long. Tim dived across the room in the direction of the doorway. His headlong dive was slowed down by the plastic tank of stick insects beside the door. The force of Tim's crash sent the light tank reeling over.

The lid had never fitted all that well.

Not surprisingly, it came off. The two stick insects he had brought home from school only a few weeks ago were now more like fifty. This mini green army continued to march in the direction it had been spilt. They swarmed towards the top step, just outside the doorway, and in seconds had disappeared.

Tim rolled over and put his head through the open door. Mum was standing, white-faced and frozen, half-way up the metal staircase, while the invading green legion slid, hopped and flopped steadily down the steep staircase towards her. Jumping jellyfish! thought Tim. Why did this have to happen now?

'Sorry, Mum!' said Tim feebly. 'I . . . err, slipped and accidentally knocked the tank over.'

Mum neither spoke nor moved.

'Hadn't you better go back downstairs—quick! You could go and make yourself a nice cup of tea while I collect all the stick insects,' he said, ever hopeful.

Mum unfroze just as the first green insect reached her feet. She bolted down the steps and straight into her bedroom, where she shut the door very firmly.

He wondered if he should reassure her that she was quite safe. That stick insects were rather stupid beasts really and hadn't learnt to open doors. But on second thoughts he decided that, under the circumstances, that would not be wise. He might not survive to be grounded until his eighteenth birthday.

Frannie stood in the hall, her head turning from her mother's bedroom door to the stick insects and back, like a tennis spectator. As the first insect jumped across her foot, she screamed, long and loud. Mum's voice was immediately heard from behind the door.

'Get those . . . those dreadful creatures picked up this instant, Timothy! Frannie, go into your bedroom, darling, and shut the door.'

But Frannie was made of sterner stuff. Once she got over the initial shock, she was fascinated by the creatures, and helped Tim round them up. But there were stick insects

everywhere. They were throwing themselves down the main staircase, invading the bathroom, and scaling the bookcase in the upstairs hall. They seemed to be multiplying even as they went. By the time he and Frannie gave up, hot and sweaty, Tim felt sure they'd collected more like a hundred stick insects in the plastic tank. He taped the lid on securely and put it carefully by the front door.

He pulled the cord that made the staircase to his bedroom fold away, and went downstairs to make Mum a cup of tea. He knocked quietly on her door. There was no sound from within.

'I've brought you a nice cup of tea, Mum. I'll put it down outside your door, shall I? I know I'm grounded, but would it be all right if I just went down to John's house? He's got three lizards, you see. I'm sure he'd be glad of the stick insects to feed to the lizards. Then they'll be out of the house forever. I'm sorry, Mum. I really didn't know they could breed that fast! A pity Dad couldn't have seen them though, I bet *he'd* be interested. It's quite amazing, how fast the babies grow up and breed, isn't it?'

Still no sound from the bedroom. Mum displayed no interest in the reproductive rate of Tim's pets.

'I guess that's OK with you then, Mum. I'll get rid of the stick insects. Don't worry, I'll take Frannie with me.'

Tim set off with the tank in his arms, a delighted Frannie at his side, and his pockets full of pennies from his money box. They soon delivered the stick insects to Tim's friend John, who was very glad to see them. Feeding three hungry lizards was a hard job.

As Frannie waved the stick insects a sad goodbye, Tim felt rather regretful about their fate. They deserved a better end after saving him so perfectly from a fate worse than death. Still, a scientist couldn't afford to be sentimental.

He took Frannie to the playpark, with a visit to the sweetshop on the way. She loved being out with Tim and couldn't quite believe her luck.

'Here's the deal, Frannie,' he said seriously. 'This is your opportunity to do me a big favour, and at the same time play a vital part in an important discovery. I'm doing some very important research in my bedroom. If I get it right I could become famous, like . . . like . . .' Tim tried hard to remember a famous person that Frannie might have heard of.

'As famous as Otis the Aardvark?' asked Frannie incredulously.

'Yes—at least,' agreed Tim.

Frannie was most impressed. 'What do you want me to do?' she asked eagerly.

Tim looked at her thoughtfully. Being four had really improved Frannie no end. She was almost human now. He got out the sweets.

'I'm sure you *do* want to help me anyway, but this is just to help you remember. You can have a tube of Smarties now, and the fruit pastilles afterwards, if you do exactly what I tell you. We're going to go home now and make a picnic for you and Mum. Then you are going to help me persuade her that you should both go out until teatime. Beg, cry, tell her how much you've missed her, do anything you like, just make sure she takes you out. Got it?'

Frannie got it right away. She took the Smarties with a cry of delight and promised to make Mum take her on a picnic, no matter what. They went swiftly home and Tim started making sandwiches at once. Pretty soon they had the picnic all packed up. He went upstairs and knocked on the door again. Mum opened it and looked nervously around, as if she expected to see the hall had taken on the appearance of a jungle, with insects of all kinds on every square inch of wallpaper.

'They're all gone,' Tim said reassuringly. 'I gave them to John for his lizards. I'm really sorry they came out at you like that, Mum. I accidentally knocked their tank over. I didn't mean to. I've made you and Frannie up a nice picnic. I thought you'd like to get out of the house for a bit. I'll get my own lunch, and carry on with what I was doing. I was . . . err, tidying up my cupboards, actually. Did you . . . err . . . notice that? I thought I might get rid of my comic collection, I'm getting a bit old for that sort of thing.'

He didn't mention that he'd agreed to swap the comic collection with John for a pair of white mice. He waited, miserably, for the bomb to drop. Had she been up there and seen it all, or not?

But Mum hadn't been about to risk going up to his room. For all she knew the gerbils were swinging across the ceiling on the light fixture like trapeze artists at the circus. The hamsters were probably tap-dancing their way across the furniture. The rat could even be chewing its way down to her own bedroom like a Channel Tunnel mining machine at this very minute.

'I think the picnic's a very good idea, Tim,' she said at once. 'But don't you want to come too? You could clean your room this evening.'

'No, *definitely* not!' he said loudly. 'I've got heaps to do. Heaps and heaps.

I'll want to read those detective stories you're getting me this evening anyway.'

'All right, then, if you're sure. But we won't be back very late. You know I don't like to leave you alone in the house for long.'

She walked past him down the stairs, picked up the picnic basket and her handbag and called Frannie. She walked quickly out the door, in case she met any stray stick insects on the way. Frannie ran after her, pausing only to whisper loudly,

'I didn't *do* anything! Do I still get the sweeties after?'

'Yes, of course,' Tim whispered back. 'Just stay out as long as you can, OK?'

He watched from Frannie's window as the car disappeared. He couldn't waste another minute waiting to see if they'd forgotten anything else. He was up his staircase and back in the roof space within seconds. Tim had brought Dad's biggest chisel with him, and used it to lever up the flat piece of board that was the trapdoor.

He pulled it up and pushed it out of the way. Next he got a long piece of thick rope but he was so scared he could hardly tie the knots. At last he got it tied firmly to one of the rafters and dropped it through the hole. His heart was thumping like a big bass drum. But he had to do it. It took only a few seconds more to launch himself through the hole and slither down the rope to the floor. He was in Mr Wizer's flat.

It was dark and dim everywhere. The only light came from the glass skylight in the front door at the bottom of the staircase. One door was open. Tim peeped in. It was obviously Mr Wizer's bedroom, neat and tidy, with the curtains tightly shut, as they always were. There was a small TV set on a table at the foot of the bed, just as Tim had expected.

Tim turned to face the other door. His heart missed a beat as he noticed a bolt had been fitted to the outside of the door. It was locked from the outside. Why would anyone lock a door like that—if it wasn't to keep someone in?

Tim's hand was shaking as he

carefully slid the bolt back. He pushed the door open slowly. There, sitting on the sofa, his eyes fixed on a big TV set, was a little dark-haired boy.

CHAPTER ELEVEN

QUESTIONS AND ANSWERS

The first thing that struck Tim about the room was the smell. The whole room was stuffy and hot, because of the tightly closed windows and curtains. The smell reminded him somehow of an old auntie his Mum had often taken him to visit when he was younger.

Tim nearly jumped out of his skin as something grabbed his leg. He couldn't help it. He yelled out loud. The little boy jumped up and regarded him curiously, with wide brown eyes. Tim hardly dared look down. Then the feeling of sharp pricks in his skin woke him to pleasant memories. He looked down incredulously to see Minty wrapped round his leg, her claws digging right through his jeans. He bent down and picked her up, holding her on his shoulder, and stroking her black fur in delight. Minty purred like a train.

'Mine!' said a demanding voice. '*My* kitty!'

The boy was leaning over the back of the sofa, his arms outstretched. Already big fat tears had started to flow down his cheeks.

Tim realised what had happened in an instant. The black cat pyjama case had obviously been the little boy's favourite thing. Mr Wizer had to get rid of it, to destroy the evidence, Tim guessed. But the little boy would have been inconsolable at the loss of his kitty. So Mr Wizer replaced it with the next best thing—Minty. Why had he waited over a week, though? Maybe for the boy to get used to Minty before taking the pyjama case away.

Tim sat down on the sofa next to the boy, with Minty in between them. The little boy immediately began to stroke Minty, saying 'My kitty, my kitty,' over and over again.

Tim felt a stab of jealousy as he saw how Minty responded. A little stroke and the cat was anybody's. Still, he shouldn't really mind. At least Minty was safe, and obviously well fed. And she was keeping the little boy happy. Tim looked around. There was little else in the room for the boy to play with. A few tattered picture books and a couple of the sort of plastic bath toys you can buy in chemists. And the TV, of course.

Sesame Street was playing on the TV. It was even later than Tim thought. He must move quickly, before Mr Wizer came home. He mustn't be caught in the house.

'What's your name?' he asked cautiously.

The boy didn't seem to be a bit frightened of him, or even surprised to see him. He just seemed to accept the fact he was there. Now Tim had to interrogate him, find out exactly what was going on.

'Kitty,' said the boy firmly. '*My* kitty.'

'I know it's your kitty,' said Tim

patiently. 'Her name's Minty. What's yours?'

'No, no!' said the boy. 'Kitty, Kitty, my Kitty!'

'OK, so she's called Kitty. That's fine by me. But what are *you* called?'

The little boy hauled Minty onto his knee, which was quite a feat, as she was almost as big as he was. He stuck his thumb into his mouth, and turned his eyes back to the TV, ignoring Tim.

Tim felt completely deflated. He had come to find out who this boy was and rescue him. But now he didn't know what to do next. Then the boy began to sing along to a song on the TV. He could certainly talk if he wanted to. He just wasn't going to talk to Tim.

Tim sighed, and got up to investigate the room. Minty raised her head and watched him intently. Then, as the boy stroked her once more, she settled down on his lap, quite content.

'Some cat you are!' he said, 'I should have got a dog instead. At least they're supposed to be faithful, man's best friend. Not like you, Minty. You're everybody's best friend if they stroke you and feed you enough. And they've certainly been doing that! You're twice the size you were!'

Although he was relieved Mr Wizer had looked after Minty so well, he was put out too. He'd grieved over his pet for ages and she hadn't even missed him! The smell came from the cat litter tray over in the corner. Minty obviously wasn't allowed out at all, in case she went home. Mum's old auntie had kept her cats in the room with her all the time too. That's why Tim had recognised the smell.

He picked up the tattered books from the floor and flicked through them, looking for clues. There were three of them, all 'Little Golden Books'. They were all unfamiliar to Tim. One was the story of Johnny Appleseed, another seemed to be about giants, called *Paul Bunyan and his Ox,* and the third looked like a Hallowe'en story.

As he looked at the flyleaf of the last book, he was rewarded. Inscribed on the page he saw the words: 'This Little Golden Book belongs to . . .' Written in

pencil on the dotted line was the one word: 'Preston'.

That was something, but it still didn't help a lot. Was he Harry Preston, Billy Preston, Joe Preston? He tried a few of them out aloud. The little boy looked up at the sound of Tim's voice and saw he had his books. He pushed Minty off his lap and came bounding over. He pulled the books out of Tim's hand.

'Mine!' he said forcefully. 'Preston's books. Preston's kitty. Mine!'

'OK, Preston. I wasn't going to take them away from you. I can see you've got little enough as it is.'

Preston! What kind of a name was Preston? he asked himself. Who'd call a little kid 'Preston', of all things?

Preston added his plastic toys and a few bits of blanket from the floor to the books, and with overflowing arms, settled himself back on the sofa with all his possessions. He added Minty to the pile on his lap, put his arms protectively round the lot and glared at Tim.

He couldn't help thinking that the little boy had guts. Tim was three times his size. He smiled at him, hoping to reassure him. Obviously satisfied that the danger was over, Preston put his thumb in his mouth and turned back to *Sesame Street.*

Suddenly there was the sound of a car pulling up in the street outside. Surely Mum and Frannie were still off on their picnic? Mr Wizer's was the last house on the street. Jumping jellyfish! It must be him.

'Bye, Preston! Bye Minty! See you again soon. Don't tell anyone I was here!'

Tim knew he had to be out of there in seconds, but his feet seemed to be frozen to the floor. He must get out before Mr Wizer came in or he knew he was as good as dead.

As if she understood the danger, Minty reached out a paw and clawed at Tim's hand. The sharp pain brought his legs back to life. Luckily, gym was one thing Tim excelled at. He was out of the door and climbing up the rope before he could say, jumping jellyfish! He pulled the rope up after him and had just pushed the heavy trapdoor back into place as the front door downstairs opened. He lay on the floor, panting with exertion and fear. He was sure Mr Wizer must be able to hear the sound of his heart beating, even through the ceiling. He lay there for what seemed like ages before he thought it was safe to start crawling slowly, silently towards his room.

It was not until he was shoving all the suitcases back into his cupboard that the dreadful thought hit him. He had definitely remembered to shut the door so Minty wouldn't get out. But he had forgotten to fasten the bolt.

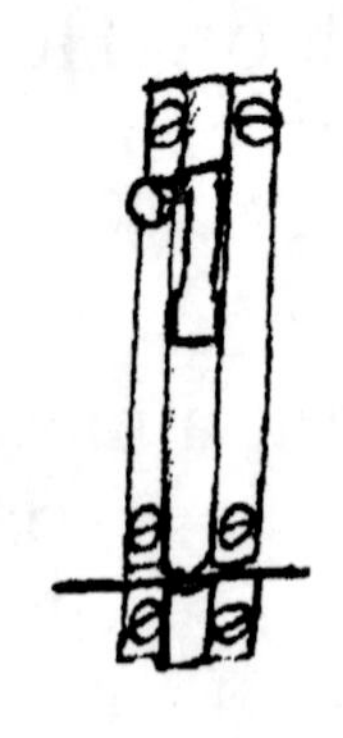

CHAPTER TWELVE

COLLABORATION

Tim spent an agonising Saturday evening expecting, any minute, to hear Mr Wizer hammering at the door—or even the police. What he'd done was illegal after all. 'Breaking and Entering', he thought they called it. That was definitely something you could be sent to jail for. He would be bound to notice that the door was unbolted. Would he suspect Tim?

As Saturday passed into Sunday and there was no sign of either police or Mr Wizer, Tim didn't relax. Far from it. At least everything would be done legally if the police came. Even if he was arrested, Mum would make sure that nothing horrible happened to him.

But even before all this happened, Mr Wizer had been out to get him. If he was as evil as Tim imagined, then heaven knows what he might do to him. If he had kidnapped this little boy and was holding him for ransom, which was Tim's theory, might not he do the same to him? Or worse—he could silence him forever.

What if Mr Wizer discovered—or worked out—how Tim had got into his flat? He could do just the same thing to Tim in the dead of night. Nobody would ever know who had murdered him. His death would remain forever as yet another unsolved mystery.

What on earth could he do? If he told Mum that he thought Mr Wizer was going to kill him, she wouldn't even listen. If he told her there was a little boy next door, she would probably think he'd imagined it—like he imagined that Mr Wizer had put his cat on the bonfire, and was murdering someone in the middle of the night. If he told her that he'd broken into the flat and actually *seen* the little boy . . . well, that didn't bear thinking about really.

It wasn't a crime to have a child in your flat, after all. Mr Wizer could just say he was the boy's father and that he was there on a visit. He always kept the curtains and windows shut, but then so did some nice little old ladies Mum knew. They were afraid the sun would fade the carpet. It's not as if the boy was tied up, or beaten or anything. While certainly not happy, he hadn't appeared dreadfully miserable either. Or only when he thought Tim was going to take Minty or his things. But weren't all little kids like that?

For a horrible moment Tim was afraid he'd just made a humungous mistake. What if it was all in his imagination? What if Preston was there for a perfectly ordinary reason, and Mr Wizer was just a very strange man who didn't like the sun on his carpets? But suddenly Dad was there in his imagination, tall and strong and reassuring.

Evidense
① Wizer - no woman or child ever seen living at Gladstone Place
② Kid locked up
- no minder.
② Kidnapp of Minty
- definitely!!!
③ Fur coat fire in garden.
Who was the woman owner ?
⑤ buried evidense
pyjama case
pyjamas
⑥ Wizer threatens me
why ?

'Look at the evidence!' he seemed to be saying. 'Look at the evidence.'

Tim looked at the evidence.

1. Mr Wizer had never had a woman or child living with him in all the time he'd been in Gladstone Place.

2. He kept the child locked in the room while he was out, with nobody to look after him.

3. He had certainly kidnapped Minty and kept her hidden in his flat.

4. He had burnt an unknown woman's fur coat in the garden.

5. He had buried the evidence connecting him to the boy—a black cat pyjama case and a pair of pyjamas.

6. He had threatened Tim.

Those six facts confirmed to Tim that there was certainly some skulduggery afoot. But he must find out more about Preston. He'd already discovered that direct questioning was no good. Preston just ignored him. He would have to get to know the child better, so he would learn to trust him. Then he might talk to him. But would that even help? Would someone as young as Preston know his own address? Frannie did, but she seemed to talk much better than the little boy. Maybe she was a bit older, or perhaps the boy was just too miserable to talk much.

Surely if he had been kidnapped it would be in all the papers. But it must have been weeks ago! If there was no news to report then the newspapers just lost interest. But he must try and get the old papers and look through them. Even *he* ought to be able to struggle through a headline about a kidnapped toddler. It would certainly be on the front page. He went to find Mum.

'Have you got all the old newspapers from the last month or so, Mum? I'm . . . errr going to do a project on headlines. You know, comparing the headlines of different papers to see how they treat the same story.'

A stroke of genius, that one. He was sure Mum wouldn't be able to resist it. Mum and Dad liked to read totally different papers. They often joked about it. And Mum didn't ever cancel them while Dad was away. It seemed too drastic a step somehow, almost as if he wasn't coming back.

'I'm so sorry, Tim. I took them to the recycling centre on the way to the library on Saturday. That was why it was so long before I discovered that I'd forgotten your library ticket. But I've got a good idea! Why don't you and Rhonda go into the library tomorrow. You can see all the back issues on microfilm now. That way you could still get your information.'

'I'll talk to Rhonda about it tomorrow,' muttered Tim, bitterly disappointed.

He'd been eleven years old for two whole weeks. If it wasn't such a struggle for him to make sense of the printed word, he would probably be reading the papers himself by now. Then he would already know if a child had been kidnapped. It just wasn't fair. If he actually asked Rhonda about them, he knew she wouldn't be content until she'd got the whole story out of him. Then he wouldn't be solving the conundrum alone.

But the more he thought about it,

the more he liked the idea. It was seriously scary being in the centre of a situation like this and wondering if Mr Wizer was going to creep in at night with a knife, to silence him forever. He must have realised about the bolt left unlocked. He *would* tell Rhonda, then at least if Mr Wizer *did* get him, *someone* would know the truth. Besides, Rhonda was really smart, and quite sensible—for a girl. She certainly wasn't the screamy, giggly sort.

On Monday morning, after an uneasy night, Tim came to a firm decision.

'Can I make a picnic for me and Rhonda, Mum?' he asked, before she went to work that morning. 'It's such a nice day. We could have it in the park next to the library. Then we wouldn't have to waste a minute of research time.'

He was hoping that Mum's offer of a trip to the library meant he was no longer grounded. It would be too difficult telling Rhonda about what he had discovered with Mrs Trump and Frannie in the house.

'Certainly, Tim, *what* a good idea. I'm so glad you're starting to be so much more positive again. Dad always *said* you were a sensible boy. But after all that nonsense with that awful man next door, I was beginning to doubt it.'

Tim felt a thrill of contentment go through him. *Dad* thought he was sensible. He would see the sense of what Tim was trying to do, if only he knew. But he was quick to pick up on Mum's comment. Mum thought Mr Wizer was an awful man too!

'Err . . . why would you say he was an awful man exactly, Mum?' he said nonchalantly, buttering buns for the picnic.

'Did I say that, dear? Oh well, maybe I did. He just seems a bit odd to me. He seems to skulk around all the time, rather as if he expected someone to be following him. Perhaps I've been watching too much TV too! It just seems a strange way for someone who's a responsible engineer to behave.'

Tim wisely said nothing more. He'd gained another piece of information. Mr Wizer was an engineer. At this moment he had no idea what earthly use this would be too him, but he was glad to know it all the same.

He was waiting out in the garden when Rhonda arrived. The picnic was in his rucksack, and Mum had even given him some money for chocolate for them both. On the way to the library he told Rhonda absolutely everything that had happened since he wrote the letter. She already knew the rest.

As he had expected, she neither gawped or squawked. She listened intently, without any comment, until Tim had finished.

'That was a very brave thing you did, Tim,' was the first astonishing thing she said. 'I think you're right. It certainly sounds like a kidnap to me. I always read the papers, but I was away in France the last two weeks before the holidays.'

Tim remembered Mrs Trump bragging about it. Rhonda had actually won the trip as a prize. She had written a very fine essay about France—in French. She was a walking, talking

French dictionary too.

'We're going to have to collaborate on this, you know. Two heads are better than one, after all.'

Tim nodded happily in agreement.

They ate their lunch in a rush, then went into the reference library to look at the newspapers. Tim was impressed by Rhonda's calm assurance in asking for the microfilms, and knowing just how to work the machine to look at them. Collaboration with Rhonda had been a great idea after all.

By the end of the afternoon Tim's head was reeling, and Rhonda too looked as if she had a headache. They'd read every newspaper for the past month—at least all the headlines. They'd looked at the papers together at Rhonda's suggestion, so they could both skim them quickly and make sure neither missed anything. But Tim knew it had been so he wouldn't be embarrassed. But there were no dark-haired, brown-eyed toddlers reported as missing.

As they walked despondently home, munching their chocolate, Tim admitted that he'd run out of ideas. He looked at Rhonda. There was a wicked gleam in her eye.

'Are we both *absolutely* sure that your Preston doesn't belong to Mr Wizer?'

Tim nodded. No real Dad would leave his own little boy alone like that.

'There's only one thing for it then.

We must rescue him! We'll kidnap him back and then find his real family!'

CHAPTER THIRTEEN

A BIG RESPONSIBILITY

Tim was stunned into silence at first. The thought was appalling.

'We can't do that!' he said at last. 'If we kidnap Preston too, doesn't that make us as bad as Mr Wizer?'

'Of course not!' said Rhonda patiently. 'We wouldn't *really* be kidnapping him. We'd be liberating him! Setting him free and returning him to his grieving parents.'

'But we don't know where his grieving parents are! Or even *who* they are! How can we return him? It's not like finding a lost cat, you know. We can hardly put an advert in the paper saying "Whoever's lost a little dark-haired boy answering to the name 'Preston', please apply to my phone number." It didn't even work for Minty!'

'That's only because wicked forces were at work. Minty had been kidnapped too—or catnapped—as she's a cat and not a kid.'

'Jumping jellyfish! This isn't *funny*, Rhonda! This isn't a game! This is a real little boy we're talking about!'

Tim had to turn away to hide the sudden tears in his eyes. He was surprised how attached he had become to the little boy. It had probably been seeing him locked up there, all alone with nothing but Minty and the TV for company. He had seemed so little, compared to Frannie, for instance. No wonder he'd been scared that Tim might take his things away.

'Listen to me, Tim. Your father's been away for ages, hasn't he? And you miss him something rotten, don't you? All of you do. But at least you know where he is. At least you know he'll be coming home in a few weeks. What if it was Frannie who'd been kidnapped? What if she'd been missing for weeks and you didn't know where she was? How would you feel then?'

Tim could say nothing. The mere idea choked and suffocated him. Was there a family somewhere feeling like that—for real—every minute of the day?

'What had you actually planned to do about him, then?' asked Rhonda.

'I don't know, exactly,' Tim admitted. 'I didn't think it would be so complicated. I thought if I just found him, he'd be so pleased to see me! He'd tell me his name and address and I'd ring up his Mum and tell her where to find him. I never thought he'd be so small he wouldn't even know he *was* kidnapped. That he couldn't even tell me who he was!'

'It's because he *is* so small that we've got a duty to rescue him. He's got nobody to help him but us! I certainly don't think about this as a game, Tim. It's more of a responsibility. An awesome responsibility. After all, if we don't help him, who will? Mr Wizer's had him for ages. That must mean something's gone wrong with the ransom payments. Maybe the parents can't raise the money. If the kidnapper doesn't get what he wants, well . . . I'd hate to think what he might do to Preston. We haven't got much time.'

Tim swallowed hard. Rhonda was right. Preston's life might depend on him. He couldn't let him down now.

'OK,' he said finally. 'We'll do it. But,Rhonda . . . how? How will we get him out? Where will we keep him? How will we find his parents?'

'Well, we haven't got the key to his house, so we'll have to get him out the same way you got in.'

'That's impossible, Rhonda! I climbed ten feet up a rope to get back into the roof space. I may be a good gymnast, but even I can't do that with a little boy in my arms!'

'Frannie showed me all round your garden the other day. I saw you had a rope-ladder going up to some old pieces of wood in the big tree. We could use that. If I held the bottom, couldn't you help him climb to the top?'

Tim felt vaguely insulted. Those 'old pieces of wood' in the tree were his tree house that he'd laboured on for many summers. Trust a girl not to recognise that. Still, it wasn't a bad idea.

'He might be able to. Frannie can climb the rope-ladder, but then she's bigger than Preston. He's such a gutsy little guy, though. I bet he could—if he wanted to. That's the big problem. What do we do if he doesn't want to be liberated? And where are we going to keep him afterwards?'

'I think the only place would be your room, don't you? I doubt if we could smuggle him out of your house without anyone seeing us. And I share a room with two of my sisters. I could never hide him.'

'But what if Mum hears him? What if he cries? How will I feed him? What do I do if he needs to pee—or worse?'

'We'll just have to speed up our investigations. We must locate his parents as soon as possible. Until then—we'll just have to treat each situation as it arises.'

Tim sighed deeply. What had he got himself into? Suddenly he had an even better idea.

'Even if we can persuade him to be liberated and come with us, there's going to be lots of times when I can't be there with him. What if he starts to cry? Everyone will hear him. Why don't I ask Mum if you can come and sleep over for a few days. She won't mind—as it's you. You can sleep on the bedchair in the study. We can tell her we're working on a special project together. Then we can try to always have one of us with him.'

'Good plan, Dr Watson,' said Rhonda enthusiastically.

Tim suddenly grinned at her. Could

she possibly be a Sherlock Holmes fan too? There was more to girls than she had imagined.

Mum was astonished at Tim's request. He hadn't invited a *girl* to sleep over since he was six years old. But Rhonda was such a nice girl. Such a good influence on Tim. He hadn't mentioned that awful Mr Wizer once since she'd been coming to tutor him. Yes *such* a good influence.

'Certainly dear, we'd love to have her! She could bring her things when she comes tomorrow, couldn't she?'

'Well, actually, Mum, we thought we could just go over to her house and get her stuff . . . if you don't mind. We have to check with her dad too, but Rhonda's sure he'll let her come. We really are anxious to get on with our project, you see.'

'Well, that's fine, if you're really so keen. I'm *dying* to hear about this project. It sounds so exciting. I'm sure Dad will be really pleased. You tell me *all* about it, and then maybe I could tell Dad about that when he phones.'

Jumping jellyfish! Tim's heart

dropped into his boots. One of the worst things about this whole thing, apart from being scared to death, of course, was the lies he had to keep telling his mum. He didn't usually tell lies. But then, there'd never been any need before. He hoped she'd understand—in the end.

'Well . . . it's actually top secret at the moment, Mum. We don't want to reveal anything until our mission . . . I mean, our project, is completed. Then we'll tell all! That's a promise. If *you* promise not to ask too many questions before we're done, that is.'

'Agreed!' said Mum, giving him a hug.

Tim felt even more guilty.

They went back to Rhonda's house, where she lived with her grandmother, her dad and her sisters. Luckily there was no trouble getting permission for Rhonda to stay over, as Mrs Trump knew the family so well. Mum looked rather amazed as they came back with Rhonda's things, an hour or so later. She stopped Tim as he staggered up the stairs carrying a small portable TV.

'Does Rhonda travel everywhere with that? Mrs Trump *did* tell me she was a bit touchy, but surely she won't mind watching *our* TV? How does she come to have her own anyway?' she asked in amazement.

Tim laughed nervously. This could be very awkward. Normal people just didn't go for a few nights' stay with their own TV.

'It's for our project,' he assured her. 'There's all sorts of good educational programmes on in the daytime, so I hope you won't mind if we watch some of them. We'll put it in my room so we don't disturb Frannie and Mrs Trump. It's Rhonda's big sister's TV anyway, but she offered to lend it. She's just off on holiday, you see.'

'I really don't want you in watching TV all day, Tim! It's not good for you, as well you know! Anyway, I've taken the day off tomorrow. I had planned to take you and Frannie—and Rhonda of course—to the Summer Fair in Central Park.'

'Can I stay home with Rhonda, please Mum? You know you said she's touchy, well you don't know the half of it! If we go to the Fair you'll be spending money left, right and centre, you always do. Ice-creams, candy floss, all those rides! But every time, Rhonda wouldn't let you pay for her, and it would be so embarrassing—for all of us. It would be better all round if Rhonda and me just stay home and get on with our project.'

'Well . . . if you say so, Tim,' said Mum reluctantly.

So things worked out even better than Tim and Rhonda could have hoped. On Tuesday morning Mum and Frannie set off for the Summer Fair. Mr Wizer left for the dockyard at 10.30 a.m. as usual. And Tim and Rhonda got ready to liberate Preston.

CHAPTER FOURTEEN

LIBERATING PRESTON

First they went out into the garden and unfastened the rope-ladder. Tim also took down three of the big planks of wood. He hadn't forgotten that unlocked bolt on Preston's door. He planned to make his bedroom a safer place. They took them all up to his room, together with Dad's toolbag. This time Tim made quite certain that the staircase was pulled up after him. That would at least give him another few seconds if Mum should come back.

With the two of them it only took a few minutes to empty the cupboard and push back the hardboard wall. They crept across the roof space and levered up the trapdoor. Tim tied the rope-ladder securely to a rafter, while Rhonda stuck her head down the hole and listened carefully. There was no sound to be heard.

Tim went first down the rope-ladder, then held the bottom for Rhonda. They both advanced towards the door in silence. Tim had a moment of panic. What if the boy wasn't there? What if Mr Wizer had already disposed of him? But the bolt was fastened. Tim slid it back and opened the door.

Immediately Minty leapt from the back of the sofa and draped herself across his shoulders like an overgrown fur stole. That was her favourite position. Tim quickly sat down beside Preston before he could start to protest. They had to keep him happy at all costs. At least liberating Preston would mean liberating Minty too.

'Hi, Preston! Do you remember me? I've brought my friend Rhonda to see you and Min . . . err . . . Kitty. Is that OK? We brought you some sweeties. Do you like sweeties, Preston?'

Tim shook the tube of Smarties

invitingly. Preston regarded him warily for a moment, then took the Smarties and imitated Tim, shaking the tube.

'The sweeties are inside,' said Rhonda. 'Let me open it up and show you.'

Preston quickly put the Smarties behind his back.

'Just let him find out for himself, Rhonda. Little kids like to shake tubes and make noises and stuff like that.'

It was nice to feel a bit superior to Rhonda for a moment. At least he knew how to deal with small children. He'd had lots of experience, but she was the youngest in her family.

'Put his stuff in the rucksack then, and let's get on with it!' said Rhonda impatiently.

She was obviously more nervous about this whole thing than she made out. For some reason this made Tim feel more confident.

'You can't rush it with little kids,' he assured her. 'We've got to get him to trust us.'

Preston had by now discovered the Smarties inside the tube, and was chewing them enthusiastically, singing away as he did so. It was a song about healthy food and healthy teeth, and too many candies giving you cavities.

'What on earth's he going on about?' asked Rhonda.

'It's a *Sesame Street* song,' said Tim. 'Didn't you ever watch *Sesame Street*? They're always singing stuff like that. They teach kids how to read and spell and cross the street and stuff, with lots of little songs. They learn everything that way. Preston's a big *Sesame Street* fan.'

Tim showed Preston the rucksack, a pink and purple affair, covered in cats and little kittens. Frannie had received a new rucksack for her birthday, so she'd been quite happy to swap last year's version for a couple of packets of sweets.

'Look, Preston, it's the *Aristocats*! Have you seen that film, all about the cats and the little kittens going on a journey?'

Preston grabbed the rucksack and began to sing the theme tune to the film. He was obviously a Disney fan too.

'Doesn't he ever do anything but sing? Can't he talk properly?' asked Rhonda.

'He says, "No!" and "Mine!"' said Tim with a grin. 'He can talk when he wants to. Perhaps he just feels safer singing songs he knows from home.'

They watched Preston collecting up his few belongings and packing them into the bag.

'Little kids love putting things into bags,' said Tim, glad that he'd remembered. It would make it so much easier getting Preston out if they had all his things together.

Suddenly there was a great squawk as Preston tried to add Minty to the collection in his bag. Preston turned to Tim and held up his hand trustingly, his eyes full of tears. There was a little scratch across the back of his hand.

Tim felt tears prick the back of his own eyes as he stretched out his arms and picked the little boy up. As the boy cuddled up against him, Tim looked over and met Rhonda's gaze. Their eyes made a solemn pact. Whatever they had to do to get Preston back home, they would do it. Tim staggered, as a very heavy cat leapt onto his shoulders once more.

'Jumping jellyfish! What are you feeding her, Preston? She feels like an elephant!'

Preston laughed delightedly. He reached up and stroked Minty, the scratch forgotten. Rhonda began to sing 'Nellie the Elephant' and Tim joined in. Preston was thrilled, and jumped up and down in Tim's arms in time to the music.

'Would you like to come and play at my house, Preston?' asked Tim softly.

'I've got lots of toys, and a TV. We can watch *Sesame Street* together soon, and sing all the songs. And I've got some more sweeties there.'

'Candy gives you cavities,' said Preston with a mischievous grin, as he snuggled back against Tim's shoulder, draping Minty's tail around his face.

'Let's go, then,' said Tim. 'I'm going to go through the floor in a minute, with the weight of these two! They must be feeding Minty lead cat food!'

Rhonda helped Preston put the rucksack on his back and they went back out into the hall. Rhonda went up the rope-ladder first, then held down an encouraging hand to Preston. Despite the huge spaces between the wooden rungs, Preston struggled manfully upwards with help from Tim below and Rhonda above. Then Tim climbed up, Minty still firmly draped across his shoulders.

As soon as they got to the top, Minty leapt off and ran across towards Tim's bedroom. They pulled up the rope-ladder and unfastened it. Then they carefully replaced the trapdoor.

'I'm just going to bang some nails in, Preston, so don't be frightened of the noise. We don't want anyone to fall down this hole, do we?'

Rhonda tried to shepherd Preston into Tim's bedroom, but he wouldn't budge. He squatted down and watched Tim intently as he nailed the three big planks across the top of the trapdoor, with as many nails as he could fit in.

'I don't think anyone will be coming up this way again,' said Tim with satisfaction, as he wiped the sweat from his eyes.

A horrible thought struck him. They should really have looked to see if there was anyone in his house before he started hammering. But it was too late now. They crawled back through the hole in his wall and, thankfully, there was nobody there. Rhonda went downstairs to get them all a drink and biscuits while Tim screwed the hardboard back in place. Preston watched all this in concentrated silence. He really seemed to be a very self-contained little boy.

Suddenly, without any warning,

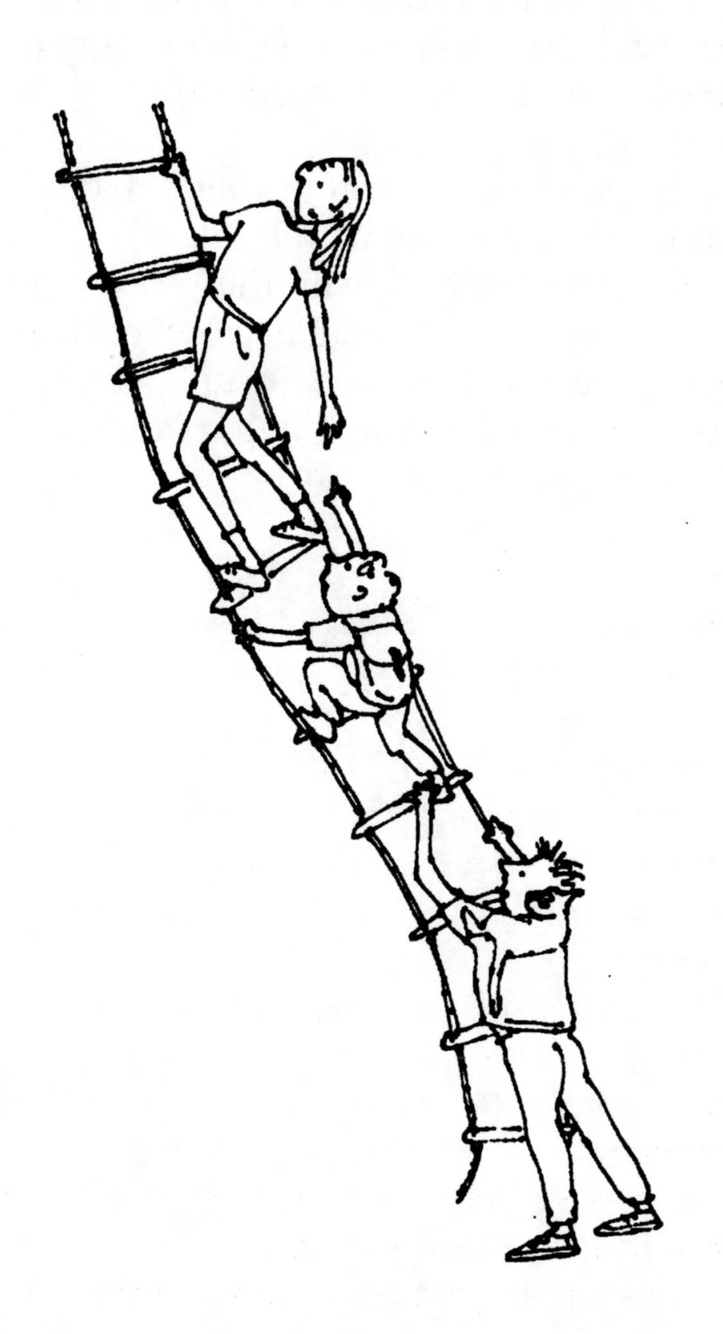

Preston's face crumpled and he started to cry. Rhonda came in with the tray of drinks and Tim turned to her in despair.

'He was fine a minute ago! I don't know what's wrong with him!'

Rhonda put down the tray and sniffed the air. 'Well, I'm no expert, as you'd be the first one to tell me. But from where I'm smelling, I would say he's just wet his pants!'

CHAPTER FIFTEEN

CLUES

'What!' spluttered Tim in disgust. 'Frannie was perfectly trained long before she was his age!'

'Ah, but Frannie is a girl, and it's a well known fact that girls develop control much earlier than boys,' said Rhonda smugly. 'Besides which, he's been kidnapped. Kids always regress when they have a traumatic experience. That means they go backwards, by the way.'

'I *know* what it means! Well then, know-it-all, just exactly what are we going to do about it? I can't have him peeing all over my bedroom!'

'*I* am going to go out and buy a pack of nappies, and *you* are going to take him into the bathroom and clean him up,' said Rhonda promptly.

'Why should *I* do it? It was your idea to liberate him in the first place. You're a girl! Girls are supposed to *like* doing stuff like that. It's part of their maternal instincts.'

'Not this one!' said Rhonda. 'Besides, *he's* a boy, and *you're* a boy. So you're more familiar with the equipment. I'll buy the nappies, as your mother just paid me for tutoring you, and you've bought all those sweets for the kids. They should have some in that little shop at the end of the road, shouldn't they? I'll be back in five minutes.'

Rhonda was gone before Tim could say another word. Reluctantly, he took Preston by the hand and led him to the bathroom. But Preston was scared of the open treads on the folding metal staircase, and refused to go down them. So Tim had to pick him up and carry him. He was soon more than convinced that Rhonda's hunch was right.

Tim stood Preston in the bath and started to peel off his clothes. They were a weird combination, not the sort even the least fashion conscious person would put together. And none of them fitted him properly. He didn't have any shoes or socks and the rest of his clothes looked as if someone had just gone into a charity, shop and selected the first small things he saw on the children's rail.

With the aid of the hand shower spray, Tim managed to get Preston clean and sweet smelling again. By the time he got him back up to his bedroom, Rhonda was back and unpacking the nappies.

'I got the biggest size. You wouldn't believe how expensive they are! You can put them on him.'

'I'm foiling a kidnap attempt here, you know, not running a creche! Just what exactly do you think I am?'

Rhonda grinned. 'I think you're a very nice big brother, of course. What's he going to wear? He can't go round draped in a towel forever. And what did you do with his wet clothes?'

'Jumping jellyfish! I left them on the bathroom floor! What if Mum had come in and found them? Never mind, you can grab them when you're down there. Mum's just bought Frannie a whole pile of new shorts and tee-shirts. The old ones are in a plastic bag in the airing cupboard. I was supposed to take them up to the charity shop, but I never got round to it before I was grounded. Could you bring them up?

I'm sure we can find him something better to wear than his old ones.'

Preston wouldn't let Tim put a nappy on him, no matter how he tried to persuade him.

'No diaper!' the little boy wailed, over and over again.

So Tim gave up and dressed Preston in Frannie's old clothes and a pair of slightly too large sandshoes. He looked a hundred per cent better than the little boy they'd liberated, less than an hour ago, even if he was dressed all in pink. Tim switched on the portable TV and settled him down to watch *Sesame Street.* As the familiar signature tune came on and Preston started to sing along, something began to nag away in Tim's mind.

It was as if there was some word just on the tip of his tongue, but he couldn't quite think of what it was. Something he almost knew, but not quite. It really bugged him, and he racked his brain, trying to work out what it was. Suddenly it came to him. Great jumping jellyfish!

'Rhonda! Rhonda, get up here

quick!' he yelled. 'I know something about Preston! I've worked it out!'

Rhonda was down in the bathroom, trying to mop up Tim's energetic cleaning operations. Tim hadn't even noticed the water all over the place, but his mum would. She bounded up the stairs and Tim drew them up to make them quite private.

'I've got it, Rhonda, I've got it!' he said triumphantly.

'Got what? Just tell me, for Pete's sake, Tim!'

'Why we couldn't find out about Preston's kidnap in the paper! It wasn't in the paper because it didn't happen in England!'

'How on earth can you know that?'

'From the clues, Rhonda, from the clues! I looked at the evidence, just like Dad told me.'

'How could your Dad tell you anything? He's not even here!'

'Don't be an idiot, Rhonda! I *visualised* what he might tell me. All the clues we've been looking at so far have been to do with Mr Wizer. What about all Preston's clues?'

'I didn't know Preston gave you any clues. I thought he could hardly talk!'

'He's said quite a few things, so far, if only we'd listened.'

'But I can't even understand half the things he says,' said Rhonda ruefully.

'Exactly!' said Tim triumphantly. 'That's exactly it! All the things he's said have been running round my brain, driving me loopy! Now I've put them together and worked out what they have in common. Listen to this: candy, cavities, diaper—a kid called Preston. What does that say to you?'

'America!' said Rhonda. 'He's an American!'

'Got it in one! Well, about half a dozen actually, but never mind. Then I looked at his little books. They were all published in America. Just look at the story titles. You know all about literature. Do they mean anything to you?'

'Of course,' said Rhonda, as she examined the little books. 'These are all classic American stories in cartoon form. Well, what do you know!'

'So now all we have to do is find out

exactly who he belongs to.'

The enormity of that hit them both at the same time.

'There are fifty states in the USA, Tim. There are over two hundred and fifty million people! How are we going to find Preston's family?'

They both thought for a very long time as Preston sang along beside them.

'Why don't we ring up a big newspaper in America and ask if there was a little boy kidnapped about two weeks ago?' said Rhonda at last. 'If there was, maybe they could tell us where it was. That would be a start.'

'Which one? I don't know any American newspapers,' protested Tim.

On *Sesame Street* they'd just finished singing the 'In Your Neighbourhood' song.

'That was a good song, wasn't it, Preston?' said Tim. 'My neighbourhood's called Mutley. Did your mummy ever tell you what your neighbourhood was called?'

'Mommy,' corrected Preston. 'My mommy. My mommy's gone.'

'We know your mommy's gone. We want to help you find her, Preston. Can you remember what your neighbourhood was called? Was it called . . . err . . . Chicago or,' Tim struggled to think of an American place name, 'or Boston . . . or what?'

'Not Boston, silly,' said Preston. *'Brooklyn!'*

'That's in New York!' said Rhonda. 'And I'm sure there's a paper called the *New York Times*. We'll phone them.'

Preston wouldn't be parted either from the TV set or from Tim, so Rhonda went down alone to find the information. First she phoned International Directory Enquiries and got the right number. Then she phoned the paper. A sleepy voice answered her. She took a quick look at the clock. It was still early in the morning in New York.

'This is Rhonda . . . err . . . Smith of the . . . err,' she took a quick look at the paper folded up beside the phone, 'of the *Guardian* newspaper. I'm looking for information about the kidnap of a child about two weeks ago . . . yes, it was in New York . . . Brooklyn, I think. Yes, I'll hold.'

Five minutes later she was still holding. I only hope Preston's mother will pay the phone bill, she thought, with a sinking heart. Then there was a crackle in her ear before the information was passed over.

Rhonda raced up the stairs.

'You were right! There were two kidnaps in New York that made the news about two weeks ago. One was a ten year old girl, but the other was a little boy who was kidnapped on his fourth birthday. Get this: The boy's name was Preston Balushi. But the police are searching the USA for the boy's father. They want him to "help them with their enquiries". That's what they always say when they suspect someone. His father is described as having dark hair, piercing black eyes and a scar across his left eyebrow.'

CHAPTER SIXTEEN

DISCOVERY

'That's Mr Wizer!' repeated Tim. 'Then Preston must . . .'

'Yes,' agreed Rhonda. 'He must be Mr Wizer's son.'

'We've just kidnapped Mr Wizer's own son! We've kidnapped Preston and his father lives right next door and he's going to be home any minute! What are we going to do?'

'Yes, but he kidnapped Preston from his mother in the first place! We only liberated him. He should never have taken him. It's still down as an unsolved kidnap in New York. Mr Wizer is still the monster we thought he was all the time. Kidnapping his own son! He must be a real rat!'

'Where's Kitty?' asked Preston.

But Minty was nowhere to be found. She'd vanished the minute Tim's door had opened. Preston's whimpering threatened to turn into outright wails any minute.

'What are we going to do?' asked Tim. 'It's not safe for Preston to stay here now. Mr Wizer will be home soon. If he starts to howl he's bound to hear him. Then he'd get in here somehow and take him back. If he disappears with him and finds another hideout, we'll never get Preston back to his mother.'

'But we have to keep phoning. We have to phone all the Balushis in Brooklyn until we get through to Preston's mother!'

'We'll have to go to your house and do it there. We can tell your Gran . . . I know, we'll tell her a friend of Mum's came over early because Mum promised to baby-sit Preston for her tonight. So we're looking after him for her, until she gets back. We'll tell her we came over because you forgot your pyjamas or something. Then we'll stay until we've got through to Preston's Mum.'

'What exactly was I supposed to have worn last night, then? It won't work anyway, Tim. Do you imagine my Gran would just sit there and let us make lots of long distance calls to New York? Well, she wouldn't!'

'What are we going to do then?'

'Well, if I take Preston back to my house as we planned, could you stay here and do the phoning? Then when you get through, you can tell Mrs Balushi to tell the New York police, and they can tell the Plymouth police. They'd listen to them.'

'Jumping jellyfish! That sounds awfully complicated, Rhonda!'

'Well, what do you suggest? If we just take him to the police station, they'll ask Mr Wizer, who'll say, "Yes! Thank heavens, you've found my son! These two terrible delinquents broke into my house and kidnapped him!" By the time they've checked out *our* story—if they even bother to—Preston and Mr Wizer will be long gone.'

Tim sighed. He hated telephones. He still sometimes wrote down the numbers in the wrong order.

'OK then. You'd better hurry. Take Preston's rucksack with all his stuff. And Rhonda, give him one of Frannie's dolls to carry. Find him a nice soft one to cuddle, as he's lost Minty. Then, with his pink outfit and all those black curls, people may think they've just seen two girls going past. That's if Mr Wizer is out looking for Preston.'

Preston was very reluctant to leave without either Tim or Minty. Suddenly Tim had a brainwave. He raced up to his room and dived under the bed, then came down the stairs three at a time.

'Kitty, Kitty, *real* Kitty,' shouted Preston with delight, as Tim thrust the black cat pyjama case into his arms.

'You go for a walk with Rhonda now, Preston, and I'll come and join you just as soon as I can.'

Preston set off happily with Rhonda and real Kitty. Tim double-locked the front door and went into the living room to continue with the phone quest.

He dialled the number Rhonda had given him for the International operator, and got to work. He had already spoken to seven Balushis in Brooklyn by the time he heard Mr Wizer's car drive up and park outside the house next door.

Tim put down the phone and ran to the window, where the curtains were billowing in the late afternoon breeze. He quickly pulled the sash down and locked it with the security key. Tim breathed a sigh of relief and went back to the phone.

If Mr Wizer had his son here for a legitimate reason, wouldn't there be police cars drawing up outside the house within minutes? The police didn't waste time when a small child disappeared. If Mr Wizer reported his loss to the police then Tim would know it within five minutes, he was sure of it.

Many minutes past. No police car arrived. No distraught father ran up and down the street, knocking on doors and asking if anyone had seen his little boy. Tim kept on dialling.

Eventually his call was answered by the voice of a tired-sounding woman. Tim asked his question for the fifteenth time,

'Is that Preston's mother?'

There was silence on the other end for a moment, then a long drawn-out sob.

'How can you torment me like this? You horrible kids have nothing better to do

than to make fun of a poor grieving mother! But you wait, I'm getting on to the operator! I'm getting your number! I'll have the cops round there before you know it! You can be arrested for malicious phone calls, you know!'

Tim had never felt so upset, or so embarrassed.

'It's not a malicious call, Mrs Balushi, really. I've been trying to find you for ages! Your son Preston's here! He's safe. He's been at my house, but now he's round with my . . .'

'Where is he? Oh my poor baby, where is he?' interrupted Mrs Balushi.

'He's in Plymouth, in England,' began Tim.

'In England! How did he get to England? Are *you* in England?'

'Yes,' repeated Tim patiently. 'This is my address, 28 Gladstone Place, Mutley, Plymouth. That's in Devon.

Can you write that down, Mrs Balushi, it's important. I live next door to your husband. He's calling himself Mr Wizer. Preston's been here with him . . . Mrs Balushi? Mrs Balushi, are you there?'

There was nothing but an ominous silence on the end of the line. Tim looked up, and saw the dark, menacing form of Mr Wizer filling the doorway.

'I knew all along it would be you,' the man said, his enormous black brows knitted together in a ferocious scowl, the sinister scar quivering. 'As soon as I found that bolt left unfastened, I knew it had to be you!'

Too late, Tim remembered the back door, and the last time he'd been through it with his arms full of planks of wood. He hadn't even shut it. Had that only been this morning? It seemed like a lifetime ago. Tim stood up. His knees were trembling.

'I'm *not* going to tell you where he is!' he said as forcefully as he could. 'Never. No matter what you do to me! You'd better go! The police are probably on their way at this very minute. They'll be here soon, and they'll arrest you for kidnapping Preston!'

'Pity you won't be around to see it then,' leered Mr Wizer.

CHAPTER SEVENTEEN

DANGER!

Mr Wizer came towards him, Tim looked round quickly for something to defend himself with. He grabbed the big telephone directory beside him and hurled it straight into Mr Wizer's face. As the man staggered from the blow, he raced past him and out of the door. Tim knew he had only seconds to escape. He'd double-locked the front door and knew he could never get it unfastened in time.

His bedroom. If only he could get up to his bedroom he could pull the folding steps up after him and be safe. He raced up the stairs, Mr Wizer only steps behind him. Suddenly he felt, rather than heard, the big man trip on the staircase. He didn't dare stop to look behind him, but hurtled on up, through the landing and round to his own metal staircase.

The afternoon sunshine streaming through the stained glass landing window made it gleam like the stairway to heaven. Never had he been so pleased to see it. Never had he climbed it so swiftly. Relief surged through Tim as he neared the top and saw his bed, his cages of pets. Even the messy piles of suitcases and cardboard boxes they'd taken from the loft space looked good to him as he reached the opening to his bedroom. Safe at last.

Tim yelled with pain as his chin came down hard on the top step. His right ankle was held in a vice-like grip and he was being pulled steadily down the staircase. Although his eyes were blurred with tears, Tim could see the evil face of Mr Wizer below him. He wrapped his arms round the top step and kicked out wildly with his free leg.

The man gave a grunt of pain as Tim's foot came in contact with his head. But he still hung on to his ankle like a bulldog, pulling the boy steadily towards him. With a yell, Tim let go of the step and leapt backwards off the staircase. Caught off guard, Mr Wizer let go of his leg as he fell backwards onto the landing floor, with Tim on top of him.

Tim staggered to his feet. Mr Wizer was between him and the stairs. Where could he go? How could he escape? In a flash it came to him. The bathroom. There was a cherry tree outside the bathroom window. If he locked himself in there that would give him time to open the window and climb out. He was sure he could manage to do it before Mr Wizer broke the door down, as he was sure he would do, within minutes or even seconds.

He'd never climbed out of the bathroom window and on to the tree before. For one thing, it had always looked a bit flimsy to bear his weight. For another, climbing out of windows and on to trees was something you only read about in books, not something children really did. For another, his mum would ground him for life if she found out! But he'd never been in a situation like this before.

He'd climb out of the tree and be through number 26's front door before Mr Wizer knew what had happened. Their phone was in the hall and he'd call the police before he even told the old couple what was happening. He'd be safe there until the police came.

His escape plan flashed through Tim's mind before Mr Wizer was even on his feet again. He dashed to the bathroom door and was through it in a fraction of a second. He was trembling all over as he slammed the door and leaned all his weight against it. As he reached for the bolt he was amazed to see that the front of his shirt was covered with blood. Automatically he put his hand up to his sore chin and mouth and pulled it away, covered with blood. He must have bitten his tongue when his chin hit the step.

The sight of his own blood suddenly brought home to Tim the danger he was in. This wasn't a game. It wasn't a detective case like Sherlock Holmes that he was trying to solve before he got to the end of the chapter and all was revealed. Mr Wizer might do *anything* to him to make him tell where he was hiding Preston. He must have cut the telephone wires so Tim couldn't call for help. That's why the phone went dead. *Dead.* Jumping jellyfish! That's what he could be soon.

Tim's knees felt as wobbly as jelly. His legs buckled and he slid down to the bathroom floor. He doubted whether he could climb out of the window. He doubted he could even shout for help out of the window. He tried yelling, but nothing came out of his mouth except air. His voice, his whole body seemed to be paralysed.

A movement in the corridor outside brought him back to his senses. Mr Wizer must have been momentarily stunned by his fall. But now he was flinging open bedroom doors, searching for Tim. He knew he had to do something quickly, or he would be caught.

His arms, feeling as heavy as lead, reached up for the bolt on the bathroom door. His hands flailed about wildly as they felt nothing. Tim staggered to his feet and gazed at the door, horror-struck. Instead of the strong, sturdy bolt, there was nothing but a patch of darker paint and four small holes.

In a flash he remembered. Frannie was a pretty sensible child, but her friends were not always as reliable. Last weekend she'd had a friend round to play and they'd managed to lock themselves in the bathroom while they were bathing their dolls. The bolt was stiff and they couldn't undo it. Mum had to get the long ladder out and Tim had climbed up it, with Mum hovering anxiously below and hanging onto the bottom. It had been easy to climb in and open the bolt from the inside. Tim longed for that ladder now.

But Mum had insisted on removing the bolt from the door. Tim never locked the door anyway, so he hadn't noticed that it was missing. Now there was no way he could escape from Mr Wizer. He tried though. He turned and climbed up onto the sink and was fumbling with the window catch as Mr Wizer crashed through the bathroom door with a yell of triumph.

'Got you at last, you little horror. You won't escape me now!'

Tim turned and faced him, trembling with fear, but still determined not to tell him where Preston was. Mr Wizer took a step towards him, his arms outstretched, ready to grab Tim and force the truth out of him.

CHAPTER EIGHTEEN

JUMPING JELLYFISH

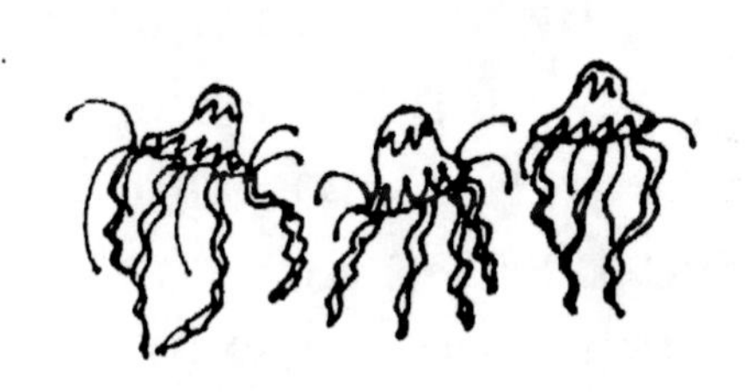

A large, heavy black shape hurtled from the top of the airing cupboard onto Mr Wizer's shoulders. The weight and force sent him reeling. As he fell, he hit his head against the corner of the bath. He lay on the floor without moving.

Tim looked from Minty to the still form, face down on the floor in front of him. He was gobsmacked. Still trembling violently, he bent down beside Mr Wizer and was relieved to find him breathing heavily.

'Jumping jellyfish, Minty!' he muttered. 'You scored!'

He reached up and pulled down a

pile of Mum's tights that were drying over the bath. He used them to tie Mr Wizer's wrists and then his ankles together. Then he ran downstairs and out into the garden and brought in the spare clothesline. He couldn't shift the heavy body, but he wound it round the man's arms, which were tied behind his back, then tied it to the feet of the heavy, old-fashioned iron bath. Mr Wizer wouldn't be going anywhere.

Tim wanted to run down to Rhonda's house and tell her that he'd found Preston's mother. But he didn't want to leave Mr Wizer here for his mother and Frannie to find when they got back from the Summer Fair. He wanted to phone Mrs Balushi back to make sure she'd got his address down before her husband ripped out the telephone cable. But he couldn't leave the house to do that either. He couldn't even risk going next door to number 26. All he could do was to keep guard and wait.

When the police finally arrived they found Tim sitting outside the bathroom door with Minty in his lap. He'd pushed a broomstick across the door and through the handle so it couldn't be opened from the inside. Mrs Balushi *had* managed to take down his address and had immediately rung the police in New York. They'd been in touch with the Plymouth police who were on the scene very quickly.

Luckily Mr Wizer didn't start to come round until just after the police arrived. Tim was worried that Minty might have killed him but the policeman seemed to think that he would be all right. It was the same sergeant who'd given Tim the telling off, down at the station.

'I have to admit, young Tim, that when we got the information and I saw *your* address on it . . . Well, I was all ready to book you for wasting police time . . . again. But it seems that your man was up to some serious skulduggery all the time,' said the policeman, getting out his notebook. 'Not that I hold with children—or anyone else, for that matter—getting involved with dangerous criminals! You should have informed us of all the facts

at the beginning.'

Tim didn't bother to point out that he hadn't known all the facts at the beginning, or that they wouldn't have believed him even if he had. That didn't seem to matter any more. All that mattered was that Preston was safe. Minty was safe. Even *he* was safe, although he'd better get his blood-stained shirt changed before Mum came home, or she'd have a fit! The sergeant took Tim's statement. This time he believed every word.

Mum and Frannie got back just after Mr Wizer was taken off to hospital in an ambulance, escorted by several policemen. Tim thought that Mum would go ballistic! But, despite her astonishment and bewilderment, she was great. They went down in a police car to collect Preston from Rhonda's. Frannie was thrilled.

'Can we have the siren on?' she demanded, much to Tim's secret delight.

So the police car zoomed across town, blue lights flashing, siren screaming.

Rhonda and Preston were out in the garden when the police car drew up. Preston immediately ran to Tim and threw himself into his arms. Rhonda followed swiftly behind. Rhonda looked at Tim over the top of Preston's dark head.

'You did it, Tim!' she said softly.

'No, *we* did it, Rhonda!' he said, hardly able to believe it himself. 'The police have got Mr Wizer. We've liberated Preston—and Minty!'

'I knew we could do it!' she said as she grinned down at him.

* * *

The rest of the day went by with a succession of visits from policemen, social workers and reporters. Mum offered to look after Preston until his mother arrived on the first plane the next day. The police and the social workers agreed, as Tim and Rhonda were the only ones Preston would go to.

Next morning Tim woke late. He sat up sleepily and rubbed his eyes, the events of the past few days still zipping through his sleep-muddled brain. He almost thought it had all been a dream. Then Preston rolled over and wedged himself against him, real Kitty still in his arms.

Tim looked around him. He had dragged his mattress down to the living room to share with Preston. Rhonda was sitting up on the sofa, where she'd slept, already awake and reading a book. Not to be left out, Frannie had also joined them with the mattress from her bed. She was still snoring softly, near Tim's feet.

He had been glad to have them all around him last night. The sound of their steady breathing, as he lay awake for a long time, had helped to chase away the memory of that terrifying time when he'd been alone in the house with Mr Wizer. He was sure it wouldn't bother him any more.

Rhonda looked up from her book and caught his eye.

'By the way, Tim, there's something I've been meaning to tell you. You know those jellyfish of yours?'

'You mean . . . the ones who ought to be undulating?'

'That's right. Well . . . I just wanted to say . . . I prefer them jumping!'

CHAPTER NINETEEN

SKULDUGGERY SCUPPERED

Preston and Frannie woke up at the sound of Tim and Rhonda's voices. For a few moments there was chaos, as pillows and sleeping bags were hurled around in a friendly pillow fight. But the noise brought Mum in from the kitchen and soon Frannie and a much less subdued Preston were taken off to get dressed.

It wasn't till after breakfast that Frannie remembered her usual early morning job, and went off to collect the newspapers and letters from the front hall.

'Look Mum, it's Tim! Tim's on the

front of the paper! Both papers! Tim and Rhonda!'

Tim grabbed the paper from his little sister. 'Rhonda, look! It *is* us!' he said excitedly. 'Shall I read it to you, Mum?'

Without even thinking about it, he managed to read out the main headlines.

SKULDUGGERY SCUPPERED
IN THE NICK OF TIME!
Two young 'detectives' risk their lives
to save kidnapped tot

He repeated the words, 'skulduggery scuppered', really enjoying their ringing sound as Rhonda scanned the rest of the article.

'It says that Mr Wizer had a new job as an engineer in some Arab country,' she said. 'He was going to take Preston off with him in only a few days time. It says our action saved Preston from a terrible fate!'

'What do they mean, "a terrible fate"?' said Tim.

'It means that Preston might never have seen his mother again if you hadn't found him,' said Mum. 'She would never have got him back, as women have no right to their children in lots of Middle Eastern countries. If his father said he had to stay with him, the law there would insist that Mrs Balushi couldn't even see her son. So you acted just in time.'

'Jumping jellyfish!' said Tim—and Rhonda.

* * *

Tim was dreadfully embarrassed when Mrs Balushi arrived from America that afternoon. She was small and dark, like Preston, but very round. With her huge voice she reminded Tim of an opera singer. She hugged him to her squashy front until he almost suffocated, saying over and over again in a rich, deep voice, 'You saved my baby, my bambino! How can I ever thank you?'

When he finally emerged, red faced and self-conscious, it was Rhonda's turn. But, being much taller, she was saved the suffocating part of the embrace. Afterwards they were both pleased to hear all the details of the conundrum they had tried to solve for so long.

'Preston was only a tiny baby when I married that rat, Wizer. His real father died before Preston was born. He was knocked down by a cab in New York City, poor guy.'

'Jumping jellyfish! So Mr Wizer wasn't Preston's real dad after all!' interrupted Tim.

'No man would treat his own kid that way!' replied Mrs Balushi, wiping away a tear. 'Preston was very quiet as a baby, slept all the time. It was as he grew older that the trouble started. My husband was always a miserable man, never liked children. Hated the noise, hated the mess. I ask you, how can you have children without noise and mess?'

Her whole body shook with emotion, as she appealed to Mum, who nodded sympathetically. Preston was already cuddled against her but Mrs Balushi reached out her free arm for the nearest child to enfold into her other side. Tim neatly sidestepped and gently shoved Frannie in her direction. With

the two little ones on her lap she continued her story.

'I thought he would feel different as he got to know Preston. But no, it didn't work out, and he left. I have to say—I was glad to see him go. I can't remember what I ever saw in him, to tell the truth! I always loved to make stuff for the kids. I made up all these cute little furry characters—a bit like the *Sesame Street* gang—but different. Before I knew it I was making them for all the big toy stores in the city, then the whole country. They were a hit! Now I have lots of women in the neighbourhood making them for me. I have a factory even, a cuddly toy factory! Who'd have thought it?'

'I'd love to see them,' said Rhonda.

'You shall, my pet, you shall! I'll send you a crate of them as soon as we get home! Anyway, when he heard I was making money he came back and demanded his share. *His* share! I told him his share was absolutely zilch! He was that mad! I knew he'd try to do something to get back at me, but I never thought even he could be so wicked as to take my baby from me!'

'I'm not a baby, Mommy,' interrupted Preston. 'I'm four now, like Frannie. Can we have ice-cream now?'

'Ice-cream! Ice-cream for everyone!' shrilled Mrs Balushi. 'These wonderful children deserve all twenty-four different flavours!'

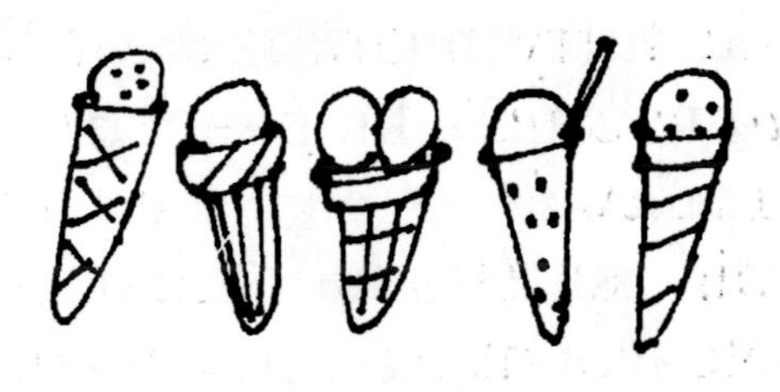

'We only have vanilla and chocolate,' said Mum calmly. 'But it *is* very hot. Would you children all like a cone?'

'You shall all come to America for a holiday! My brother owns an ice-cream company. He makes twenty-four flavours. You'll try them all! I'll show you America! What do you wanna see?'

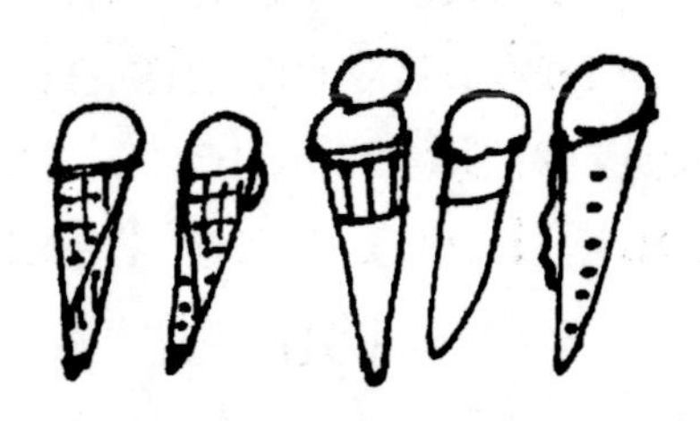

'Disneyland!' yelled Frannie immediately.

'Frannie!' said Mum, Tim and Rhonda together.

But Mrs Balushi crushed Frannie to her, ice-cream and all, and promised them Disneyland and so many other treats that Tim's head began to spin at the thought of it.

'You were telling us how Mr Wizer—your ex-husband—kidnapped Preston,' he prompted.

Mrs Balushi nodded and carefully wiped away the ice-cream that was dribbling down Preston's chin.

'He's not even ex. We never got divorced. That's how he could take Preston and keep him. In his country Preston and I actually belonged to him! Because I wouldn't give him the money, he crept in one night, wrapped Preston in my fur coat, and abducted him. He didn't want him. It was simply to get his own back at me. Preston always zipped his little books inside Kitty, once he'd taken his pyjamas out, and he always cuddled it all night through, so that's how he had them with him. He was on his stepfather's passport as well as mine, so it was easy for him to get straight on a plane and fly to England. It's not unusual for little children to travel in their pyjamas on a night flight, so nobody remarked on that. So if Tim hadn't seen that rat trying to destroy the evidence, he might have got away with stealing my baby.'

'Do you know why he came to England?' asked Tim eagerly.

'He told me once he'd worked in Plymouth before. He's an engineer, he's worked all over. But I never thought he'd come to England! They've been looking for him in the Middle East, where his family came from.'

'From what the police say, he won't be going anywhere for a good long time,' said Mum.

By the time Preston and Mrs Balushi went home, a few days later, Tim had got used to her booming voice and expansive manner and was really starting to like her. He'd perfected a good method of avoiding most of her constant embarrassing hugs without hurting her feelings, usually by shoving Frannie in instead of himself. He thought his little sister really deserved her place on his reward trip.

* * *

Tim had a lot of things to tell Dad when he came home a few weeks later. One was that his paired reading with Rhonda had gone so well that he had now read nearly the whole of a Sherlock Holmes story by himself. Another was the prospect of a family trip to America next summer—with Rhonda, of course. But the first, and most important thing, was that Minty had just given birth to five kittens in the airing cupboard.